Pieces for the Left Hand

Also by J. Robert Lennon

Pieces for the Left Hand

100 Anecdotes

J. Robert Lennon

Graywolf Press

Publication of this volume is made possible in part by a grant
provided by the Minnesota State Arts Board, through an appropria-
tion by the Minnesota State Legislature; a grant from the Wells Fargo
Foundation Minnesota; and a grant from the National Endowment
for the Arts, which believes that a great nation deserves great art.
Significant support has also been provided by the Bush Foundation;
Target; the McKnight Foundation; and other generous contribu-
tions from foundations, corporations, and individuals. To these
organizations and individuals we offer our heartfelt thanks.

Published by Graywolf Press
250 Third Avenue North, Suite 600
Minneapolis, Minnesota 55401
All rights reserved.

www.graywolfpress.org

Published in the United States of America

ISBN 978-1-55597-523-4

6 8 10 12 14 13 11 9 7 5

Library of Congress Control Number: 2008935605

Cover design: Kyle G. Hunter

Cover art: Paint-By-Numbers Collection, Archives Center,
National Museum of American History, Smithsonian Institution

for Steve Murray

Contents

Introduction

The author of these stories is forty-seven years old. He lives in a renovated farmhouse at the edge of a college town somewhere in New York State, with his wife, a professor at the college. He is unemployed, and satisfied to be unemployed, and spends an inordinate amount of time looking out the windows at the road and woods and the orchard at the bottom of his hill. He shaves once a week, is always showered before 8:00 a.m., and takes long walks daily, regardless of the weather. He cooks all the meals and does all the cleaning; indeed, he believes he is a better cleaner than the professional one he dismissed when he lost his job. He considers his solitude to be a great and unexpected gift to his life, and in fact occasionally finds himself regarding it with a kind of moral superiority, which he swiftly quashes, but not without a moment of amusement at his own vanity. The author is often amused by his faults.

What he did for a living isn't important—if you were to talk with him for a hundred years, he would never even bring it up. It was the kind of job most people would call tedious, and so would the author, except that its particular tedium appealed to him, insofar as it busied his mind and protected it from worry. It supported his family when his wife was in graduate school, and now that it is gone, he doesn't think about it at all.

Instead, he walks. Some days he walks for hours, cutting through fields and forests, hiking along the shoulders of roads. Local people, initially wary at his appearance, have grown used to it, and now they smile and wave when he passes. He enjoys imagining what they must think of him, this idle member of the middle class. He likes to think that they find him odd, though he is aware that there are too many people like him in this town for anyone to think that.

Some time ago, these walks began to shake things loose in the author's mind. Dark memories of his childhood—his mother's misery, his father's death. He began to remember events he had witnessed, stories he had heard, thoughts he had had that he couldn't let go. Things that happened to his neighbors, to his wife's colleagues. Things he read in the paper. Every day, for many months, he sifted through the growing pile of memories, until he had begun to tell them to himself, as stories. I once knew a man, the stories began. A woman I know. In our town. The stories accumulated, forming a script in his mind, a repertoire. Some of them are true. Some have been embellished, or fabricated entirely. If he had to, the author could get up on stage and recite them all, but this isn't the kind of thing it would occur to him to do, or that he would enjoy. What he enjoys is being alone, telling himself stories.

The stories are there now, in his mind, as he walks. He is happy with them the way they are: ephemeral, protean. In

2

time his mind will move on to other things, and he will forget them, or most of them. Eventually the author will probably find a job—he isn't bored, but he senses that he will be, and he would prefer not to taint with boredom these excellent days.

JRL

1. Town and Country

For more than a century, the main street in our town was named after a founding father of our state, a man who, in a recent revisionist essay, was revealed to have been a corrupt, bigoted philanderer who beat his children and disliked dogs. After a string of protests disrupted rush hour traffic, our mayor took down the street signs and promised to rename the street. But loyalists protested the removal, and the signs were restored. Further protests again eliminated the signs, and the battle has moved to the courts. Meanwhile, our town's main street has no name at all, confusing visitors, complicating mail delivery, and making us the butt of vicious joking from other, less volatile neighboring towns.

Dead Roads

It is not unusual in our area for a road to fall into disuse, if the farm or village that it serves should be abandoned. In these cases, the land may be taken over by the state for use as a conservation area, game preserve or other project, and the road may be paved, graveled or simply maintained for the sake of access to the land.

But should the state find no use for the land, the road will decay. Grass will appear in the tire ruts. Birds or wind may drop seeds, and tall trees grow; or a bramble may spring up and spread across the sunny space, attracting more birds and other animals.

In this case, the road will no longer be distinguishable from the surrounding land. It can then be classified as dead, and will be removed from maps.

Election

Our town's electorate, generally quite active in, even obsessed with, local politics, was silenced during this year's mayoral race, in which the two prominent candidates, an incumbent Republican and a Democratic challenger, conducted campaigns of such a vituperative and vengeful nature that few city residents bothered to show up at the polls. Life might have gone on as usual afterward had not a nineteen-year-old college freshman, a hotel management major with no political experience, entered the race in the eleventh hour as an independent, registered six thousand students to vote, covered our town with cheaply xeroxed campaign posters reading STOP THE BULLSHIT, and published an editorial in the newspaper advocating the elimination of a city ordinance forbidding the sale of alcohol before noon on Sundays. The student's victory was a landslide.

It all seemed like a good joke until I saw our former mayor, disheveled and dark-eyed, buying a six-pack of beer at a neighborhood grocery one Sunday morning. After that, my own failure to vote seemed a terrible mistake, and I was filled with a shame and dread that linger still.

The Current Event

When I was young, our quiet city suffered the most painful disaster of its history: fourteen teenagers fresh from a party secretly boarded a boat belonging to one of their parents, brought it out to the middle of the lake, became drunk aboard it and, in the sudden storm that followed, capsized and drowned. The subsequent public grieving, underage-drinking crackdown and lake-safety campaign were covered in our local paper with sensitivity and insight, by a reporter whose fine writing and acute perceptiveness of current events I had known when we attended high school together.

When recently three fishermen drowned in a similar boating accident, the same reporter covered the current event as skillfully and thoroughly as he had covered the previous one. I happened to encounter the reporter around this time, and commended him on his efforts, which commendation he seemed pleased to receive. But when I pointed out the parallels between this incident and the other, he grew puzzled and asked me which incident I meant. Surprised, I reminded him of the drowned teenagers, and at last he nodded in recognition.

I could not resist telling him that it seemed odd that he would not remember, while reporting on a boating accident, the worst boating accident in the history of our town, which he himself had reported on at the time. In reply he only laughed and said that the previous incident, tragic as it had been, was presently "off his radar."

Claim

A local Indian tribe, irritated at the state's reluctance to issue it a permit to open a gambling casino, dug deep into its historic archive and unearthed a long-forgotten treaty granting it a large parcel of land which consisted not only of the area generally recognized as their territory, but also of a small spur, bounded by and including two creeks, on which our beloved three-term Democratic senator happened to own a summer cabin. The tribe's announcement of their intention to reclaim this land was met at first with puzzlement, then derision, as many state residents owned land there and enjoyed hunting, fishing, cross-country skiing and snowmobiling within its borders. Nevertheless, a respected state judge declared the treaty legal and binding, and in a terrific political victory for the tribe, the state reconsidered its permit refusal. Ground for the casino was soon broken, and tribal leaders made a verbal agreement not to act on their land claim.

The casino was a smash success, drawing tourists from hundreds of miles away, and the controversy died quietly. Then, during an election-year stump speech near the reservation, the senator out of nowhere berated the tribe for its now-moot threat, and declared that only over his dead body would any greedy Indians wave their tomahawks upon his family's land. The statement's overt belligerence, coupled with its reckless ethnic stereotyping, rekindled tribal interest in the land. This time, however, tribal leaders were backed by a number of liberal political groups and a considerable fortune in casino profits.

The treaty became the focus of a political campaign characterized by endless sniping and overblown rhetoric, and when the election was over, the senator had lost his seat to an anti-tax conservative with broad appeal over an ethnically diverse constituency. The tribe immediately began legal proceedings to win back their land, and within six months had recovered more than 70 percent of it, with the state paying minimal compensation to displaced landowners evicted from their homes. The senator is now roundly despised statewide, and lives anonymously with his family in another part of the country.

When asked, while walking down the state house steps mere days after the election, what had made him issue his fateful statement, the senator could not answer. In a now-famous gesture, he shielded his eyes from the sun and shook his head ruefully, then slowly let fall his hand until it covered his face, and refused to remove it until reporters left his presence.

Opening

A discount department-store chain hoped to open a retail outlet in our town, and identified a site, on the edge of the city, where it preferred to build. The site lay at a bend in a creek, opposite a popular town park prized by both naturalists and recreationalists for its broad shade trees, clean water and abundant wildlife.

The town council, eager to bring new jobs to the area and stimulate economic activity, immediately agreed to allow the chain to build, on the one condition that they choose a different site for their store. The park, the council explained, was too valuable to the community to mar its beauty with commercial development. The chain took offense at this condition and called in its legal team, who filed a series of suits, tying up the town's attorneys and emptying its coffers with breathtaking speed. Ultimately the town gave up and issued the chain its permit, and the store was constructed quickly, using contractors from a neighboring state and laborers trucked in from the city.

For its opening day, the new store ordered several thousand butterflies to be released on the site, as a means of generating publicity and demonstrating its commitment to the natural environment. However, it was July, and the air conditioning in the van that was to deliver the butterflies broke down. The van driver, a temporary worker ignorant of the insects' needs, thought nothing of the problem and arrived uncomfortable but on time at the new store.

The company's CEO had taken a particular interest in this store, and now spoke in the parking lot to a crowd of reporters and eager consumers about the company's virtues. Then, with a wave of his arm, he ordered the butterflies released.

Sadly, the butterflies had suffocated in the blistering summer heat. Undaunted, the CEO sent his employees into the store for fans, which were unboxed, plugged in, and deployed within minutes at the edge of the parking lot. These employees, mostly local teenagers, scooped handfuls of the insects from their plastic bins and flung them into the path of the fans, where they fluttered artificially for some seconds before coming to rest on the hot pavement.

The few customers who entered the store after this debacle tracked butterfly innards down its aisles, leaving long green stains on the white tiles. Those who left were forced to use their windshield wipers to clear the butterflies from their cars. The entire spectacle was captured in words and pictures by the journalists present. Nevertheless, the store has been an enormous success, as it has been in most towns, and many regard the CEO's performance with the fans as a perfect example of the resourcefulness and creativity that have made him the retail giant he is.

Copycats

Our town is famous for its deep, beautiful mountain gorges spanned by one-lane bridges, and it is from these bridges that local would-be suicides typically jump. On a recent bright October morning, a young man, a student at the university, was found dead at the bottom of a gorge by two hikers. Police discovered in the student's dormitory room a torn scrap of paper on which were scrawled the words

can't

go on

and the death was ruled a suicide. This news was a great shock to the student's friends and family, who knew him as fun-loving, even hedonistic, and much was said about how you can't truly know anyone, and how each of us, ultimately, is alone in the world.

In the days that followed, a rash of copycat suicides ensued, each with his own scrawled suicide note explaining that he too could no longer go on, and that it was only the first student's decisive act that convinced him there was a way out. Further misery and mourning overtook the community and high fences were promptly erected atop the bridge railings.

Not long afterward, the original suicide's roommate returned from a vacation and presented to police the rest of the paper that the suicide note had been torn from. Restored, the note now read:

> Midterms over, dude! I totally can't
> wait for this party. You can go on
> without me if I'm late.—B.

Around this time police also discovered the suicide's hat caught in the branches of a tree growing in the gorge, and a scrap of fabric caught in a bramble which matched the suicide's ripped pants. They theorized that the student had attended a party, gotten drunk, lost his hat in a gust of wind and fallen to his death attempting to retrieve it.

Though still in mourning, the young man's family was consoled to hear that their relative had not been so unknowable after all. However, the parents of the copycats have sued the police department and are expected to be awarded more than fifteen million dollars in damages.

Town Life

A small town not far from here gained some small notoriety when a famous movie actress, fed up with the misanthropy and greed of Hollywood, moved there with her husband, children, and many dogs and horses. In an interview published in a popular national magazine, the actress said that she was sick of being recognized by tourists on the street, approached by scheming strangers at restaurants, and generally restricted in her activities by her own popularity. The nearby town, she said, offered ample privacy and a beautiful natural setting; most importantly, she added, she would not be bothered there by slimy, self-interested people more concerned with what she represented than who she was.

Hearing this, the denizens of the small town resolved to make her residence pleasant, and agreed they would welcome her in the same way they would welcome anyone who moved there; that is, the chamber of commerce sent her a package of advertising circulars, her neighbors engaged her in lively debates about the borders of her property, the police solicited her for tickets to the annual charity ball, and she was encouraged in town to apply for shopping club memberships, coffee punch cards and home improvement loans.

Respectful of her fame and her unwillingness to acknowledge it, the townspeople averted their eyes when she passed them on the street and made no mention of her films, which everyone of course had seen. When her new movie debuted, the town filled up with reporters and photographers, but all requests for comment on the actress were rebuffed, and a few dedicated townspeople even claimed to be unaware that she lived there. The local paper printed no articles about the national press presence, and ran only a short wire-service review of the new film.

Not long after, a terrible scene erupted in the diner when the actress threw down her utensils in the middle of an otherwise unremarkable meal and shouted something to the effect that the townspeople were the unfriendliest bunch of stuck-up bastards she'd ever encountered. Within weeks she had sold her enormous house in the hills and returned to California.

The nearby town is still baffled by her strange behavior. As for the actress, she has said nothing about her experience in our area, except that she was unaccustomed to town life and was glad to be back where she belonged.

Rivalry

Autumn, once the most popular season in this town of tall trees, is now regarded with dread, thanks to the bitter athletic rivalry between our two local high schools. The school in the neighborhood commonly called the Flats is attended by the children of the working class, who are employed by the town's restaurants, motels, gas stations and factories, and who live in those low-lying areas most frequently plagued by pollution, flood and crime. The school in the Heights, on the other hand, is populated by the children of academics and property owners, who live on wooded hillside lots that offer panoramic views of our valley. Students at the Flats consider students at the Heights to be prissy, pampered trust-fund halfwits, while Heights students regard Flats students as mustachioed, inbred gas huffers. Historically, these class tensions were brought to bear in the annual football game, played at our university's enormous stadium the last weekend in October.

Five years ago, however, some Heights players spray-painted ethnic slurs on the dusty American sedans of several Flats team members, and the Flats players retaliated by flinging bricks through the windows of the shiny, leased sports coupes of their rivals. Four years ago a massive mêlée at a fast-food restaurant landed players from both teams in the hospital. Three years ago the much-painted "Seniors' Rock" in front of Flats High was rolled into a nearby creek, and the brand new sciences wing of Heights High was set on fire. Two years ago each coach was kidnapped by still-unidentified members of the opposing team and traded on Friendship Bridge at midnight of game day; and last year the Flats' beloved mascot, the Marauding Goat, was disemboweled before the war memorial in Peters Park, while not a mile away the starting quarterback for the Heights was partially paralyzed in a hit-and-run incident outside a drive-up bank. The subsequent game was canceled.

This year's game has also been canceled, but for a different reason entirely. A steep drop in the population of our town has made the existence of both high schools fiscally untenable, and beginning with the fall semester the two will be combined into a single entity, to be called Area High. It remains unclear how the rivalry will play itself out, but many seem convinced that the solution lies in targeting a common enemy, such as the students of nearby Valley High, thought by all to be buck-toothed hicks, or those of faraway City Regional, who everyone knows are greasy-haired gang-bangers. Meanwhile the peace here in our town remains uneasy, and we await with trepidation the turning of the leaves.

Get Over It

Eager to escape the pressures of life in a large town, we spent the night in a village between the lakes, at a bed-and-breakfast we had selected from a travel brochure and which, in all its particulars, seemed to suit us perfectly. But when we spoke with its proprietor, an elderly man with dyed black hair, we found him extremely unpleasant. His manner was lethargic, and he mumbled, and seemed caught in the grip of a deep depression.

When we ventured into the streets, we encountered other villagers as grim and uncooperative as our host: the man at the newsstand failed to respond to our greeting and gave us the wrong change; the waitress at a lunch counter ignored us for quite some time, then sighed loudly as she served our food; and a police officer refused to direct us to a pay telephone.

At last we discovered an ice cream parlor, its corner storefront brightly painted with whimsical designs, which was attended by a cheerful young man in a paper hat. We made small talk with the young man, and after a few minutes asked him why everyone in town seemed so glum. He told us there had been a fire that had claimed the lives of eleven schoolchildren, and that the village, consequently, was in mourning. He himself was from a neighboring county and hadn't been around for the fire.

This information cast a pall over our weekend in the country, and we returned to our bed-and-breakfast tired and dispirited. In the morning we felt bad for condemning our host and his foul mood, and so, while checking out, we apologized, promising to return at a less trying time.

Our host seemed puzzled. It didn't matter when we came, he said; the fire had happened forty years ago. When we asked him why everyone was still so miserable, he became angry and asked us to leave.

Driving home, we too became angry. Forty years, we decided, was more than enough time to get over it. Today the village strikes us as weak and stubborn, and we have not returned.

Composure

Our recently unseated mayor is again in the news, now that a certain incident related to his failed campaign has come to light. During the last month before the election, in a highly publicized and truly ambitious stunt, the mayor visited every house in our town, distributing pamphlets and soliciting questions and comments regarding his past term of office. In a neighborhood near the university, our newspaper reports, the mayor encountered a young woman, a graduate student in semantics, who asked him in, offered him a piece of cake and a cup of tea, then invited him to her bedroom, where, she contends, she locked the door and began to berate him about his suburban development policy.

According to the student, the mayor had already unbuckled his belt and was beginning to unzip his trousers when she made clear her true intentions. The mayor denies that he had begun to undress; he insists that he only went upstairs to help the student find some photocopied environmental impact reports she had misplaced and which she needed in order to make her point. At any rate, the result of the student's ploy was a noisy argument heard by several neighbors, which, according to the student, ended in the mayor's physically assaulting her, and, according to the mayor, ended with his agreeing to address her concerns in an upcoming zoning board meeting, and her grudgingly releasing him from the room.

The case is now under investigation, and public opinion, though not at all supportive of the student's tactics, is nonetheless in favor of her version of events. My own sympathies, for partisan reasons, are also with the student, though I recall that the mayor canvassed our neighborhood that same day, and that I spoke to him less than two hours after the alleged encounter took place. I remember him having been perfectly composed, answering my questions clearly and with genuine interest. Whether this composure was evidence of a clean conscience or of a monstrous emotional detachment and moral corruption remains to be seen.

Silence

A friend from the city lived for some years in a basement apartment situated directly over a busy subway line. Because of the excessive noise, our friend's rent was very low, and over the years he grew accustomed to, even enamored of, the trains' deafening rumble as they passed during the night.

Recently the city undertook a massive subway reconstruction program, and the tunnel beneath our friend's building was retired from regular use. Soon his landlord caught wind of the change and promptly raised the rent to a level far outside our friend's meager budget.

However, our friend tells us that he is relieved to have been ousted. The silence in the apartment, coupled with the knowledge that an empty tunnel lay mere yards from his bed, terrified him; and when, after the reconstruction, he would hear the scrabbling of a rat, the dripping of water after a storm, or the rustlings of a vagrant, the import of the sound was absurdly magnified and seemed to represent an urgent threat. He is presently seeking a new apartment in the vicinity of some other subway line, so that he might again have, at long last, a decent night's sleep.

The Pipeline

Our local university, faced with the problem of prohibitive summer cooling costs, announced a curious solution: water, they suggested, could be pumped from the perpetually cold bottom of our town's famously deep lake, diverted two thousand feet through a giant pipeline to the hilltop where the university stands, and run through a series of smaller pipes in classroom ceilings, where it would cool the air before flowing back into the lake. The project would be called WACA (WAter-Cooled Air) and was slated for completion within two years.

Dozens of protests from environmentalists and recreationalists ensued, with scientists from both sides of the issue debating the possible effects of the project. But the university had deep pockets, and the project went through against all objections. Enormous trenches were dug in the hillside, disrupting traffic and marring the serenity of many local neighborhoods, and massive pipes four feet in diameter were laid and connected.

It was not long, however, before a small group of undergraduate hydrologists examined the pipelines and discovered that the campus end, which was not yet connected to the series of pumps that would bring water to the buildings, lay exposed and open behind a chain-link fence near the cafeteria; and that the lake end, which had not yet been connected to the submerged section of pipe, lay exposed and open about ten feet above the lake's placid surface. The implications were obvious. The students rigged a fleet of wheeled pallets, donned helmets and swimsuits, and embarked upon a series of high-speed joyrides down the pitch-black pipeline that culminated in violent and exhilarating ejection into the water below.

This behavior continued undetected until the students, nine of them altogether, vanished from their summer classes. They had been missing several days when a fellow student, privy to their pipeline antics, suggested that police check the WACA sites. As it happened, WACA contractors had sealed off the bottom of the pipeline, at last connecting the submerged section to the section buried in the hillside. The students' bodies were discovered lodged in the main pump, five hundred feet below the lake surface.

The tragedy has stopped the WACA project indefinitely, and window-mounted air conditioners are once again visible jutting from the ivy-covered walls of campus buildings.

Leaves

We live in a profusely and variously foliated area, and our trees are large and old, cultivated here by an excellent public works department, so it is not surprising that our town draws tourists from far away come fall, when the leaves change color. They drive through our residential streets with their out-of-state license plates, pointing out to one another the extraordinary colors, from the stunning reds of the red maple and black oak to the orange of the birches and radiant yellow of the gingko, a streetside specialty here. Occasionally a visitor will pull over and compliment us on the beauty of our leaves, but none of them ever thank us— for fertilizing the soil, for keeping insects at bay, for treating the wounds caused by storms, and droughts, and old age.

And then, when the tourists return to their own towns, our leaves grow drab, they fall off our trees and into our yards and gutters, and if we don't get rid of them they sit there and turn black and wet under the snow. Nobody comes to look at them then. We walk through them in our boots on the way to our cars and try to forget what's happened, and we endure the winter, and eventually the city comes and takes the leaves away. We do our best to put them out of our minds, to enjoy the bleak view of the valley between the bare branches of the trees.

The one saving grace of all this is the spring, when new leaves arrive. They've never yet failed to do so. They start out tiny and green, like mint candies, and for a short time they are ours alone, and nobody else's. And then in summer, even when wind and rain and hail tear through them, even then they stay right on the trees and make a sound like applause, all summer long. As if they are thanking us for spending this time with them before the tourists come and take them away.

2. Mystery and Confusion

Owing to the inefficiency of our plumbing, I am obliged not to wash the dishes while my wife is taking a shower. And because we have only one telephone line, I am unable to make calls while my wife is corresponding via e-mail. Therefore, today, when my wife was in the shower, I felt that I should not use the phone.

Shortcut

One night, when I was young, I fell asleep while driving down a Midwestern two-lane county highway and woke suddenly to find myself on a wide, empty interstate in a powerful thunderstorm. I pulled off the road and waited until the rain stopped, then drove to the next exit, where I found a motel and checked in for the night. I was met the next morning by bright sunlight and a feeling of disorientation, because, although the sleep had refreshed me, I had no idea where I was. A glance at the telephone book in my room reminded me that I was in Iowa. This mystery solved, I went out to the cafeteria adjoining the lobby of the hotel and sat down to eat breakfast.

Seats were scarce, so when a young woman asked if she could join me, I was happy to oblige. I engaged her in conversation and soon realized we were headed in the same direction. Since she had been stranded here by a bout of engine trouble, I offered to drive her the rest of the way. She accepted.

By the end of our trip, the young woman and I had fallen in love, and within a year we were married. Now we live together in another part of the country, our children moved out and nearing the age we were when we met. The story of our meeting in the Iowa motel is told often to guests, and occasionally we retell it to one another, for sentimental reasons.

That morning, as we climbed into the car together, I

recalled the sudden change in the highway and weather the previous night. When I'd gotten settled behind the wheel, I consulted my map to see where I'd gone wrong. I was at first puzzled, then horrified, to discover that the road I'd been driving on was practically parallel to the one I'd exited after the storm, with as many as sixty miles separating the two. In order to switch from one to the other, I would have had to make several connections on unfamiliar country roads, which might have taken more than ninety minutes. I had no memory of this drive, and could not have known how to accomplish it without careful study of the map. Nonetheless, I appeared to have done so while sleeping.

When, years later, I finally told my wife, she dismissed out of hand my version of events and insisted that I must simply have found a shortcut.

Witnesses

Our friend moved to the city and took an apartment with two acquaintances in a rough but inexpensive part of town. On the day he arrived, he witnessed, along with his new roommates, a drive-by shooting. A vehicle pulled onto their street, a gun was pointed out its window, and a young man on their block, a recent inductee into a street gang, was shot in the leg.

The police arrived and brought the three to the station for questioning. Each was taken alone into an interrogation room and later released. When they were able to meet again, our friend expressed his relief that they had gotten such a clear look at the incident; the perpetrators were almost certain to be caught. He then reconstructed the incident as he had seen it: a black Pontiac Firebird with out-of-state plates pulled onto their street, the African-American driver leveled a handgun at the young man and fired it, then the car squealed down the block and made a left turn, out of sight.

However, one of our friend's roommates objected strenuously to this version of events. He insisted that the car was a red sport utility vehicle with a bent rear fender and in-state plates, that the race of the shooter could not be determined, that the gun was in fact a hunting rifle, that the car turned right, not left, and that the squeal of tires our friend had heard was actually a scream of pain from the victim, who lay bleeding on the sidewalk.

The other roommate sheepishly admitted that he had seen

33

a white man in glasses fire a semiautomatic out the window of a rusted blue Volvo without plates of any kind, which had gone straight down the street through several lights before vanishing into traffic. He also said that he himself had screamed, which may have accounted for the noise our friend heard.

The discussion metamorphosed into an argument, which in time would evolve into a web of grudges that would never be forgiven.

When our friend, a year later, left the city to return to our town, he told us that he had done so not out of concern for his safety, as many assumed, but because he was tired of not knowing what was going on.

Switch

One night, while our cat was curled up on my lap, placidly purring, I noticed that his collar was somewhat crooked, and in the process of righting it I happened to catch a glimpse of the identification tag that hung from it. The tag, a worn stamped-metal disc, told me that the cat's name was Fluffy.

Our cat, however, was named Horace. Reading further, I discovered that the tag bore not our permanent address, but an address on our old street in a faraway town we had lived in temporarily.

I gave the matter some thought, and concluded that there were two possible explanations. One was that, while we were living in the faraway town, our cat's collar was switched with another cat's, perhaps as some kind of prank. The other was that we had accidentally gotten hold of someone else's cat and abandoned our own.

Initially I dismissed the second possibility, as it had been five years since we lived in that town, and this cat had very much come to seem like ours, and the town we lived in permanently his rightful home. But as I reflected, I realized how very unlikely a prank the switching of collars was; and simultaneously I began to recall changes in our cat's personality around the time of our move which, quite naturally, we assumed to be consequences of the move itself, but which now suddenly seemed like the consequences of his not being our cat.

On impulse, I got up and called the phone number printed

on the tag. A woman answered. I asked her if she had lost a cat named Fluffy, and after a long pause she replied that yes, she had, many years ago, and did I have some information about him? I told her that I had found his collar, unconnected to any cat. Did she want me to send it to her? After a dramatic pause, the woman told me to go ahead and do so, and I did the next day. I also ordered, through a pet supply catalog, a new tag with the name Horace printed on it.

Though I no longer consider this to have been a cowardly act, I went through several weeks of self-doubt at the time. As for now, I can only hope that the original Horace was taken in by a kind family.

The Wristwatch

While walking, on a cool day in late spring, over a bridge spanning one of our town's mountain gorges, I checked the time. At that moment, my watch band broke, and the watch tumbled from my grasp and out of sight.

Three weeks later, a pair of acquaintances invited us to go canoeing. We drove to their weekend cabin on the lake just north of town, where we shrugged on our life jackets and readied a pair of boats for launch. While paddling through calm water along the shore, I spotted something shining in the mud beneath the surface. Convinced it was my watch, I leaned over to grab it, nearly pitching my wife and myself into the lake. But my effort was successful, and I soon held the object, rusted and caked with silt, in my palm. It was a bottle cap.

That evening we all sat around a campfire, chatting and enjoying the fresh air. When the chill of night set in, I put on my sweatshirt and found the watch in the front pocket. It had fallen there, not into the creek.

Underlined Passages

While visiting a used bookstore, a man who had suffered a run of bad luck bought a paperbound work of philosophy, hoping that a new paradigm for looking at the world would help him turn his life around. He brought the book home and studied it carefully, underlining key passages with a ball-point pen. The new ideas were indeed helpful, and he grew happier in both his marriage and his work, rediscovering skills he had forgotten he possessed and generally changing his outlook for the better.

One evening, while gathering old items for a yard sale, he discovered in a dusty cardboard box a stack of books he had read years before, when he was a student. Among them was another copy of the very work of philosophy he had recently bought and that had changed his life. When he opened the older book, which he had no recollection of ever having read before, he realized that he had underlined exactly the same passages that he had in his new copy. It occurred to him that if he had absorbed these ideas in the past, and they eventually gave way to the miserable period that had preceded reading them the second time, then it was inevitable that he would enter another, similar, period of ill fortune and despair, and in fact at that moment he began to sink into a depression that would only widen and deepen in the months to come.

Eventually he and his wife grew apart and they filed for divorce. Over several wordless days they separated the possessions they had shared for so many years, and soon he moved into an apartment.

Shortly before the divorce was to be finalized, the man discovered that he had somehow retained both copies of the fateful book, and in the process of throwing them out noticed that the older copy bore his wife's name on the inside front cover. He realized that the dusty box had not contained his books from college, but his wife's, and that he could not recall reading the book the first time because, in fact, he hadn't.

He quickly phoned his wife and they agreed to call off the divorce. They are now in counseling, working to understand their new circumstances.

The Mary

A job I had one spring could be reached easily on foot through parks and residential neighborhoods, and so, in the months I held the job, I saw the same scenery twice daily, and came to enjoy imagining the lives of the people whose houses I passed. One house gave me particular pleasure, as in its backyard stood a weather-beaten white statue of the Virgin Mary, balanced on top of a round red picnic table. I liked the slapdash presentation of the Mary, and fancied that the house's inhabitants were pious in a rough-edged, practical way, unconcerned with the trappings of high-minded, pompous religiosity. In my mind, these were people of substance, not of fashion, which is how I liked to see myself in those days.

But this impression was shattered when summer came, and when passing the house I saw that the Mary had been replaced by a large canvas umbrella, and the table covered with empty beer cans and snack bags. In the same mental breath that I registered this change, I realized that there had been no Mary, only the furled umbrella whose folds, in my self-aggrandizing mental state, I had mistaken for the draped vestments of the Virgin. The house was not owned by a religious family, but more likely rented by a group of sloppy college students.

After this epiphany, my menial office job no longer seemed like the honest living I'd convinced myself it was, but a humiliating waste of time without any redeeming features. It was not long before I quit.

Intruder

When we came home, I sensed a difference in the house. A book I had been reading on the sofa now lay on the kitchen table. There was the smell of a candle lit, then blown out. A bottle of beer I'd finished drinking but left on the desk was now standing in the sink.

My instinct was that there had been an intruder. But I dismissed the possibility: we had not been gone long, and those items that had been upset were not the sort of things that would have interested an intruder. More likely, I had upset them myself and forgotten.

But in that case, there had been an intruder after all: the version of me that had done these things. Or perhaps the real intruder was the version of me that noticed the change. This made more sense, since the house as it was belonged to the version of me that had made it so, and the version of me that did not recognize it was a stranger.

The difference was that the intruder would take up permanent residence in the house, and its true owner would never return. Then it must be so, because I am still here.

Trick

A famous magician, best known for the television specials on which he caused boats, airliners and even entire buildings to vanish, was accused of the murder of one of his assistants, a beautiful young woman of twenty with whom he was said to have been having an affair. Many of us awaited the trial eagerly, for the young assistant was a local girl made good in show business, and her death a tragedy for us all. What was worse, she had been stabbed to death with a dagger and, in what appeared to be a horrible kind of magician's joke, cut in half.

On the morning the trial was to start, our newspaper reported, the prisoner was led into the courtroom by armed guards and seated next to his counsel, a prominent defense attorney whose sharp tongue and encyclopedic knowledge of the law had earned him fame almost as great that of the celebrities and business leaders he defended. All in the gallery were surprised, however, when the magician's attorney immediately raised an objection. The prisoner who had been brought into the courtroom was not, the attorney insisted, the magician. A closer examination revealed this to be true. Though this man looked something like the magician—the same neat beard, receding hairline and jutting brow—he was clearly someone else. There was considerable confusion while the bailiffs tried to find the accused and those in the courtroom attempted to learn who, if not the magician, this prisoner was. Further chaos erupted when it was announced that the accused could not be found, and that his proxy had not, until that very morning, been a prisoner at all. In fact, he had gone to bed at home the previous night and awakened in the magician's prison cell.

After taking pains to prove his identity to the authorities, the man told his story. He had turned in just after his dinner, complaining of a sudden and irresistible exhaustion, and fell deeply asleep the moment he climbed into bed. Those gathered in the courtroom began to surmise that the magician had somehow had the man drugged, and then managed to switch places with him during the night.

It then occurred to the man that his wife was still at home, and might be in danger. Police arrived at their house to find the woman unharmed but unable to remember anything she had done for the past several days. The couple lived in the country nearly a hundred miles from the prison, without pets or children, and the nearest neighbors reported no unusual activity during the night. No further clues were discovered. After a few months reporters stopped bothering the couple. Our town, meanwhile, digested the bad news and got on with our lives.

No one has yet discovered how the magician was able to make the switch, but all agree that it seems to have been some sort of trick.

Crisis

A priest of our acquaintance occasionally suffers a crisis of faith, and at these times we often encounter him in a local bar. He sits on a stool watching himself in the mirror behind the bar, and drinks steadily until he has mastered his dilemma. Then he returns to the rectory and sleeps well into the next afternoon.

One recent evening he described his newest crisis: he was unsure of the true nature of sin, and how it related to his ultimate salvation or damnation. He explained that he had, in the past, broken one or more of the ten commandments, and in the wake of his transgression begged the Lord for forgiveness. For instance, he had of late taken the Lord's name in vain upon smashing his thumb with a hammer, coveted an attractive young parishioner, and bought a lottery ticket, which he supposed was a kind of idolatry. After his penance, however, he wondered if the Lord really had forgiven him. If He had, then what was the point of the commandments? Surely they had no meaning if breaking them could be forgiven so easily. On the other hand, if he wasn't forgiven, then his damnation was certain, and there was no good reason to follow them to the letter anyway.

He wondered, then, if this very soul-searching was a form of absolution, and if so, did his opportunistic awareness of that fact negate its effectiveness? And of course it was possible that this very awareness of the possible value of the soul-searching represented an honesty and integrity that the

Lord might well appreciate. Which is to say that the ascetics and saints were either truly blessed, the only people who would get into heaven; or, they were trying much harder than they had to and consequently were fools.

It is worth noting that we have seen our friend the priest at the pulpit from time to time, and neither his message nor his delivery is in the least bit inspiring. However, when we see him at the bar, he is charming and thought-provoking, and in the wake of these encounters we always report guiltily to church.

Twilight

Employment is scarce in our town, and for a time, when I was young, I made ends meet by working as a clerk in a coffee shop.

During the summer, the town draws its share of tourists, particularly from France. We have something of a literary reputation, and some of the French are said to compare it to Paris's famous Left Bank, where writers and artists lived and worked in the early part of the last century. One afternoon I was washing tables after the lunch rush when a small crowd of tourists walked in, glancing impatiently about and speaking quietly to one another in French. Soon one of them approached me and asked a surprising question in hesitant English: Where was twilight?

I told them that they were in luck, because sunsets in our town were particularly spectacular. I suggested they walk out to the inlet and go to the end of the pier there. Look west, I said, when the sun goes down behind the hills; the heavy summer air would intensify the light so that a marvelous palette of colors would be cast onto the bottoms of the clouds and reflected on the water below.

They listened politely to my description, then a man stepped forward and, in more convincing English than his companion, explained that his friend was looking for the *toilet*. Embarrassed, I pointed the way.

Later that evening, when my shift was over, I walked home along the lake and saw them out on the pier, watching the sun set. I stood watching them watch until it was dark.

Familiar Objects

There are things I see and seek out and touch so frequently that they take on an iconic degree of familiarity, such as my wristwatch and keys and wallet. I look for these items so often that I begin to see them even where they are not: my keys appear in a pile of broken windshield glass in the gutter; a gleaming quarter spied between the slats of a picnic table takes the shape of my wristwatch; my wallet can be found in a woodpile.

I see my watch and keys and wallet wherever I go, even in places I am visiting for the first time. I see them whether or not I am actually looking for them, even if I have them on my person. The part of my mind in charge of searching for them has searched so often that it has become a separate and independent entity, always alert and at work.

This part of my mind would love for my wallet, watch and keys to be everywhere at once—for duplicates of each to be spread across every surface and wedged into every crack and crevice—so that I could take note of them and be reassured at all times. But there is another part of my mind, the dominant part, that recoils at such a thought.

Because this latter part is dominant, I am sane. But should the former part gain the upper hand, I would become mad, believing that those familiar objects were always everywhere around me.

Fingers

A friend told me about a traumatic memory he has of his childhood. In the house where he grew up, and where his father still lives, there is a hole in the floor in the corner of the living room, drilled there to allow passage to the cellar of a steam pipe which was removed when the house was converted to electric heat. This hole allows a narrow view of the cellar below. My friend recalls hearing, at about age five, his father at work downstairs with a power saw. He peered down through the hole just in time to see his father slip on some poorly stacked boards and inadvertently slice off two fingers with the saw, the index and middle of the left hand. He remembers his father's howl of pain and the spatter of blood on his workbench, and the subsequent arrival of an ambulance.

I have met my friend's father, and he is indeed missing those fingers. He has a habit, when speaking, of rubbing the stumps on his forehead.

When, in middle age, this friend shared his recollection with his father, the older man told him that he had lost the fingers in an industrial accident at the factory where he worked, and backed up this version of events with a yellowed clipping from the company newsletter, which described the incident and commented on his recovery and return to work. The father also pointed out that his workbench was not below the hole in the living-room floor and never had been, and that had such a thing happened he would not have called for an ambulance, but bound the wound and drove himself to the hospital. Furthermore, there could have been no poorly stacked boards in or around his work area, as he was unfailingly tidy and cautious with his tools. He suggested to my friend that maybe he was remembering the ambulance that brought his mother to the hospital, where she died of heart failure at an early age, and conflating it with the slaughter of some rabbits, which he, the father, had raised in cages in the cellar during the lean times of my friend's childhood.

My friend eventually came to believe his father's explanation, but he says that the memory of the severed fingers remains clear in his mind, and is all the more disturbing to him now that it appears to be false.

Plausible

I got up once in the middle of the night and went out to the street in my robe, where I saw giant yellow machines, bought by the city for the purpose of clearing wet leaves from the gutters, slowly trawling the curbs with their red lights flashing. Their engines made a throbbing noise, and if I closed my eyes I could imagine that they were tanks, occupying our town at the close of a long, hopeless war.

As they passed me I peered into the cabs and was surprised to discover no one was driving them.

On a break at my office the next day, I called the department of public works and asked if there had been street cleaners at work during the night, and I was told there had been. But when I asked if the machines had possibly been operating without drivers, I was promptly cut off.

The only other unusual thing was that it was early December, and bitter cold outside, and I recall being quite comfortable without a coat, and the sidewalk warm beneath my bare feet. Otherwise, the dream was entirely plausible, and I am still not certain it didn't happen as I remember it.

Lucid

Our dinner guest, a self-taught expert on so-called "lucid dreaming," which refers to those dreams so sensually detailed that they are indistinguishable from reality, and which, at least in our friend's case, can be created and controlled at the whim of the dreamer, arrived with an ashen face and his right arm in a cast. During the meal, we asked him what had happened, and he told us, his eyes tired and voice heavy, that he had quit the dream-experimentation for which he had become so well known.

When we pressed on with our inquiries, our guest recounted his story. He had dreamt that he was in line at the post office, waiting to mail an elephant-shaped package wrapped in brown paper. As he waited, a circus clown came dancing in the door, followed by a monkey wearing a fez and carrying a concertina. The clown distributed balloons to all the postal clerks, and then the monkey played the concertina while the clown sung an unintelligible song.

Lucid dreamers, our guest interrupted himself to tell us, have a standard "reality test," which they use to assure themselves that they are dreaming: the dreamer passes his hand through a solid surface, and this impossibility confirms the dream-state. When he reached the counter, our guest administered his reality test, plunging his own hand into the hard countertop. The impact broke two of his fingers. As it happened, he had not been dreaming; in fact, he was mailing a stuffed toy elephant to his niece, and it so happened that one of the postal clerks had that very day turned forty, and the others had hired the clown and monkey to perform a birthday song in German, a language, they explained to our pain-racked friend, often used by the clerk for comic effect.

The incident had convinced our guest to give up his beloved pastime. However, his lucid dreaming has persisted. Only the control he once exerted over the dreams has been lost. Consequently, he has no means to escape what have become terrifyingly realistic nightmares, and his sleep has been profoundly unrestful.

When another guest asked him why he wasn't certain that the entire experience of his disenchantment with lucid dreaming was not itself a dream, a wild look came into his eyes, and he thrust his bandaged hand into the dining table. The remainder of the evening was spent in the emergency room.

Virgins

The brief hysteria that overcame our town last year began when an elderly churchgoer, emerging from a morning mass, noticed that the colorful knitted scarf draped around the neck of a passing homeless man seemed to bear, in its variegated threads, the image of the Virgin Mary, and that, furthermore, the Virgin's two crudely stitched eyes appeared to be secreting tears. The homeless man was quickly surrounded by amazed parishioners, and interrogated about the origin of the scarf.

It seemed that the man had been given the scarf by its creator, a plump, middle-aged woman, during the weeks before Christmas, though she had not told him her name. A search was promptly mounted for the mystery knitter.

But before she could be found, new Virgin sightings were reported: a weeping face chiseled into the weathered serpentine of a campus building; a sad, wizened countenance growing among the knots and twists of an old sycamore, its eyes dripping sap; a sobbing icon revealed in the whorls of ice that covered the lake. Indeed, Virgins seemed to be popping up everywhere, to such an extent that, according to rumor, representatives from the Vatican were on their way to confirm the miracles.

Before they could arrive, however, the scarf-knitter appeared and insisted that she had woven no Virgin Marys into the scarves she distributed to the region's homeless over the holidays. The tears, she reasonably theorized, could easily have been melting beads of snow or ice. And as for the other sightings, she suggested, you could find Virgins anywhere, if you looked hard enough.

This seemed a cynical position to many, until a competing gallery of Jesus Christs was discovered and documented, and then a series of Moseses, and finally a suite of Donald Ducks. For some time now, townspeople have been reluctant to take anything at other than face value.

Twins

In college I knew a young man and woman, twin brother and sister, remarkable for their affinity: they were both slight, blond-haired and handsome; spoke with the same emphatic rhythm; walked with the same confident, long-legged stride; and liked the same music, food, art and film. They finished one another's sentences and were adept at games of pantomime, during which it sometimes seemed each could read the other's mind. The two were inseparable, and could occasionally be persuaded to tell the story of how their birth parents were killed in an auto accident, and how they came to be adopted by the dean of our college and his wife. They had been a campus fixture since their infancy, and were well known and loved by students, faculty and staff alike.

When they were about to graduate, the twins were gravely injured in their own auto accident. Though they survived, it was discovered in the hospital that not only were they not twins; they were not even related. Repeated blood tests confirmed this fact, and the story briefly became a national news item of the "strange but true" variety. After a few years, however, the story vanished, as did the twins.

Many years later I learned, from a mutual acquaintance, that the twins had married. They invited most of their closest friends to the wedding, but few came, or even responded to the invitation. According to my acquaintance, who did attend, the dean and his wife were not there either.

Though my acquaintance saw nothing morally wrong with the twins' union, she reported that their first dance together after exchanging vows was a shocking sight, and one she would never forget. The twins danced face to face, holding each other with passionate intensity, the line between them like a mirror that reflected everything but their gender. No one joined them on the floor, for that dance or any other.

The twins send out a family newsletter every year, complete with photographs and news. They have adopted a number of children of various races and nationalities, but have had none of their own. There is no consensus among their former friends about whether this is due to some fertility problem, or if it represents a final taboo that not even the twins themselves dared break.

Indirect Path

For many years a large table stood in the center of our dining room, blocking the most direct path from the living room to the kitchen and necessitating the development of an angled walking route that, over time, came to be visible as an area of wear in the dining-room rug. Recently we discarded the old rug and, since our children have grown and moved away and we now eat our meals in the kitchen, transferred our large table into storage. The dining room has been turned into a study, with bookshelves lining the walls and a narrow desk facing the front window.

Despite these changes, we find it nearly impossible to take the newly created direct path through the room, and continue to walk around the edge as if the table were still there. When occasionally one of us must enter the forbidden space, either to sweep the floor or to pick up a dropped item, we find that we wince in discomfort, as if anticipating a painful crash into the missing table.

The Bottle

Last summer, a bronze sculpture was stolen from the Square, a pedestrian mall at the center of our town. The sculpture, a full-scale rendition of a mother nursing her baby, had been bolted to a wooden bench that stands beneath a dogwood tree, and for some time had served as a lunch-hour companion to downtown office workers, a plaything for children and a symbol of our town's perception of itself as an open, nurturing community. At least once a year the sculpture appeared in the local newspaper half-buried under snow, or covered with fall leaves, or basking in the dappled sunlight of spring.

Though it was quickly established that the theft had occurred between the hours of two and four on a weekday, no one reported having witnessed the crime, and the investigation quickly fizzled out. How the thief managed to remove the sculpture in broad daylight, when the Square was filled with people, remained a mystery to police.

A year passed, during which most townspeople grew accustomed to the sculpture's absence, and many forgot about it entirely. Then, one recent morning, the sculpture reappeared. Police told the newspaper that they had narrowed the time of its reappearance to somewhere between nine and eleven, again when the Square was filled with pedestrians; and again no one claimed to have seen the thief. But no one could mistake the change that had been made to the sculpture: the baby, once chastely giving suck to the mother's breast beneath a fold of her blouse, was now quite clearly portrayed as drinking its milk from a bottle.

Police interrogated everyone in the area who had access to a bronze-casting facility, but none would admit to having altered the sculpture or could offer any suggestion about who else might have done it. Several of the artists questioned did admit that they admired the chutzpah of the thief, despite their disapproval of his stunt. The mayor's office quickly issued a statement supporting breast-feeding in general, and local mothers' right to perform it in public. The original artist, now dead, has been honored with a commemorative postcard. And the police have declared that anyone with information about the crime should contact them immediately. Soon, however, the incident will be largely forgotten, and few will remember that the sculpture was ever different.

The Hydrangea

We took many photos on our summer trip to a popular vacation spot, and when we returned, we brought the film to a processor to have it developed. At home, looking over the photos, we realized that they belonged to someone else: a plump couple in their thirties with two small children. They too had gone on vacation, and could be seen engaging in various recreational activities, gamely smiling at the camera.

As we were putting the photos back in their envelope to return them to the processor, we noticed something familiar in one of them: a curving stretch of beach that ended in a distinctive craggy overhang. On closer examination, we realized that the photos had been taken in the same oceanside tourist town we had ourselves visited.

We wondered if the chubby family had been there at the same time we had. Excited, we scanned the photos for evidence. One was of a large white coastal hotel that we recognized as the very one we had stayed in.

My wife reminded me that our balcony, which faced the beach, was for some reason the only one with a potted hydrangea sitting on it. The plant had obviously been forgotten by the staff, and we watered it daily to keep it alive. This hydrangea, with its large white blossoms, was easy to find in the photo, and to our astonishment, a thin, tall man wearing white socks and a red shirt could be seen pouring water into the plant from an ice bucket. It seemed certain that the man was me.

We returned the photos as planned, but kept this one for ourselves. When we were given our own photos, we searched them for the now-familiar other family, but they were no-where to be found.

A Dream Explained

As a child, and until I was a young man, I was plagued by minor infections and common colds that sometimes persisted for weeks and, especially during the winter, seemed to follow on each other's heels with almost no healthy days in between. Occasionally a fever would accompany one of these illnesses, and if the fever lasted into the night I would invariably have the same dream.

In it, I was standing alone on an undulating desert or beach. The sand below me was brightly illuminated, but the sky itself was utterly black, with no apparent source of light. I bent down and picked up a single grain of sand, and as I examined it, it fell from my grasp. When the grain hit the ground, every grain of sand was instantly transformed into an enormous boulder several times my size. I realized then that it was my job to find the grain of sand I had dropped, a task made all the more difficult now that the scale had changed, and as the dream ended I began the arduous climb over the endless field of gray boulders.

I seem to remember a hill as well, but my suspicion is that the myth of Sisyphus, which features a hill and a boulder, has tainted my memory of the dream.

A possible explanation of the dream is a trip I took with my boy scout troop when I was very young. We were to go to a place called Ringing Rocks, and were each instructed to bring along a hammer. Ringing Rocks proved to be a field of boulders, much like the one in my dream, except encircled by trees. The boulders were supposed to contain an unusually high percentage of some metallic ore, so that they rang when struck.

I remember being terribly disappointed. I'd expected the rocks to peal more sharply than they did, and I was not convinced that they were any different from ordinary rocks; so far as I could tell, most of the ringing was coming from the metal heads of the hammers.

The image I most powerfully recall is that of my fellow scouts, fanned out across the boulder field in their green uniforms, monotonously pounding, and the dull sound they made, like prisoners in a quarry with their pickaxes.

3. Lies and Blame

A tree that grows on the property line between our land and our neighbors' land for years served as a playground for the children of both families, and was happily considered a shared asset, to be maintained and enjoyed by all. But recently the tree was uprooted during a storm, and crushed a passing car. The resulting lawsuit has led to a property dispute, a flood of certified letters and the complete dissolution of our friendship.

The Manuscript

A local poet of considerable national fame completed a new collection of poems that had, due to a painful and scandalous series of personal problems, been delayed in editing and publication for some years. When the revisions were finally finished, the poet typed up a clean copy of the manuscript and got into his car to bring it to the copy shop for reproduction.

On the way, however, the poet was pulled over for running a red light and was subsequently found to be drunk. Due to a new and unforgiving drunk-driving law in our state, his car was taken from his possession and his license revoked.

Upon regaining sobriety, the poet realized that his poetry manuscript was still in the car and asked the police to return it to him. The police, however, maintained that the contents of the car no longer belonged to him, and refused. Their refusal resulted in a protracted legal battle, during which our beloved poet died, leaving uncertain the fate of the manuscript.

But the poet's publisher, eager to issue a posthumous volume, struck a bargain with the police department: if someone at the station would read the finished poems over the phone, an editor could transcribe them and issue them in book form without the manuscript changing hands. After all, the publisher argued, even if the manuscript legally belonged to the city, its contents did not, as they were devised outside the poet's car. The police agreed to this scheme, the phone recitation took place and the book was issued to great acclaim, assuring the poet a place in the literary canon that he had not enjoyed in life.

Eventually, however, the poet's estate won its legal battle against the city, and the original manuscript was recovered. We were shocked to learn that it bore little resemblance to the published book.

It was not long before a city policeman confessed to having improvised much of the manuscript during its telephone transcription. His only explanation was that he saw room for improvement and could not resist making a few changes here and there. Almost immediately the policeman was asked to leave the force, and the acclaimed book was completely discredited. The true manuscript was published in its entirety, to tepid reviews.

The policeman has continued to write poetry. Most agree that it is excellent, but few will publish the work of someone known to be so dishonest.

The Belt Sander

With our mail came a thick personal letter addressed to our neighbor. I might have acted immediately, dropping the letter into his mailbox while he was not at home. However, I had, some weeks before, lent him thirty dollars, which he had promised, and failed, to repay by the week's end, and which I wanted back as soon as possible; so, intending to visit him in person to ask for the money, I held on to the letter.

But later that day I remembered a book our neighbor had lent me almost a year before, which I had not returned because I found it self-aggrandizing, opaque and in poor taste, and had not wanted to have to lie to him that I liked it, when in fact I had not been able to finish it.

This reminded me that our neighbor had borrowed my belt sander when he moved in five years before, and never returned it. But my having forgotten this fact called attention to my own reluctance to undertake household projects requiring the sander, and I was filled with self-disgust.

The following morning I tossed the letter and book into the fire and bought a new sander, ignoring the least expensive model in favor of the one costing exactly thirty dollars. Why this choice should make me feel morally superior to my neighbor is unclear; nonetheless that is the way I feel.

Film Star's Dog

Some months ago we visited our friend the painter in the city. Over lunch he told us that it was his habit to walk his dog in a certain park near his home, and that lately he had encountered there a famous film star and her dog, which his dog quickly befriended. Owing to the dogs' relationship, our friend and the star entered into a cordial one as well. To keep the star's favor our friend kept the conversation on the subject of dogs, believing that an acknowledgment of her fame, or in fact any mention of the film industry or suggestion of his fandom, would insult her and end their informal friendship, which he enjoyed. He told us that she had recently related the harrowing story of her dog's near-death by rattlesnake bite in the mountains of southern California, and in fact the dog seemed to be in recovery from some illness, its fur patchy and its skin bright red, as if it had been scalded.

Not long after, we noticed a wire-service article about the star in our local newspaper. The article repeated the story of the snakebite and reported that the star had told it on a recent episode of a late-night talk show.

We found this funny, since it was a corroboration of our friend's surprising story, but it wasn't long before it occurred to us that our friend might have seen the talk show and invented his own involvement, for our amusement. We wouldn't have put this past our friend, who led a mysterious and solitary life and was known for flights of fancy, but since he had recently suffered a bout of mental instability (he had reportedly had a fireplace installed in his home for the sole purpose of flinging paintings into it), we resolved not to confront him about the possibility.

In the end, however, our curiosity got the best of us and we sent the article to him without any note of explanation. We have not heard from him since.

Justice

A famous and wealthy retired judge moved to our town and bought a huge, stately downtown mansion. The mansion was surrounded by wonderful grounds, consisting of lush lawns and enormous spreading trees, which in previous years had been used, with the full permission of the friendly town magistrate who used to live there, as a kind of public park, available for all manner of recreation and enjoyment.

However, the new owner had a tall iron fence erected around the perimeter of the grounds, hired men to cut down all the trees and installed a giant private pool and a four-hole golf course, which additions he could be seen, through the iron bars, enjoying in solitude. In a feature article on the front page of our newspaper, the judge described his beloved collection of Cuban cigars, and responded to our complaints with the assertion that the house and the land it stood on were his alone, and that he alone would control all activities that took place in and upon them.

Not long ago a rumor circulated that the squirrels who once lived on the wooded grounds had, in the absence of trees, taken up residence in the judge's mansion, and had found their way into his humidor and shredded his beloved cigar collection. The newspaper, eager to curry favor with the town's wealthiest resident, printed an unsigned editorial denying the rumor, but we all happen to know the town exterminator, who insists it is true. We are pleased to learn that he has been careful not to kill *all* the squirrels, because although he cannot scoff at a client of the judge's stature, at the same time he has, after all, a well-developed sense of justice.

Encounter

While walking alone one night on a deserted street in the city, I noticed a middle-aged man approaching from a block ahead, a tall African-American wearing a suit and carrying a thin briefcase. My initial instinct, given the time of day, the absence of other pedestrians and my general unwillingness to engage others when alone, was to cross to the other side of the street and avoid any encounter. But I questioned my own motives. Would I cross to the other side, I wondered, if this man, like me, were white? Perhaps not. This possibility filled me with guilt, so I resolved to remain on the same side as the man, convinced I could erase my discriminatory instincts by acting consciously against them.

When I met the man, he stopped and asked me for the time. I gave it to him. Then he asked, in a polite tone, if I lived nearby. He had no money for the bus, and wondered if he could use my telephone to call for a ride. I told him that I was sorry, but I was from out of town.

His face told me that he thought I was lying, in order to avoid bringing a black man into my home. In fact, I was telling the truth, but I wondered: would I have lied, had I lived nearby, for the very reason he had suggested? I didn't think so, but since I would have been a different, perhaps more cautious, person entirely if I lived in this neighborhood, there was no real way of knowing. To preclude further misunderstanding, I quickly offered him money for the bus instead.

The offer made him even angrier, and he asked me did I think that every black guy I came across was a panhandler? Of course not, I said. But his refusal to accept the money got me thinking that perhaps he really was some kind of swindler, maybe a clever criminal in the guise of a modest businessman, who did, in fact, want to get into my house and rob it. I would lead him to the phone, and then he would turn and pull a gun out of his briefcase.

I glanced at the briefcase, then back at his face. He shook his head, called me a honky bastard and went on his way.

Of course, had I lived in the neighborhood, this final gesture would have filled me with remorse, forcing me to let him into my house after all, where, humiliated, I would or would not have been robbed.

The Letters

A stranger dropped dead in front of the post office. Nobody knew him and there was nothing anyone could do, so the ambulance was called and passersby waited with the body as sirens approached.

One bystander noticed that the dead man was clutching a pile of stamped letters in one hand. Wishing to be helpful, she took the letters from the dead man's hand and dropped them into a mailbox. A few other bystanders nodded approvingly, while others glared as if in reproach. Still others had no visible reaction. In any event, the ambulance arrived, the man was pronounced dead and the body was taken away to be identified.

As it happened, the stranger was from another town, and had stopped in our town while fleeing his family and job. The letters had been addressed to several friends and relations, and confessed to a number of shocking betrayals which included romantic affairs, dishonest business dealings and lapses of confidence. Those who received them were horrified, and their good memories of the man they had known were tainted.

Not long afterward, the bystander who mailed the letters was successfully sued in civil court for damages related to the emotional distress inflicted upon the dead man's family and friends. The family and friends agreed that the bystander had not written the letters; nor had she caused to be mailed any letters that the dead man would not have wanted mailed himself. In fact, the dead man's family and friends admitted that they would have done the same thing had they been the bystander. Nevertheless, if it hadn't been for the bystander's act, they might have been spared the knowledge the letters contained, as the dead man's wife, upon reading them, would probably have destroyed the letters and left secret their grim revelations. The bystander, a city employee, was unable to pay the full amount of the suit, and so her wages will be garnisheed until the balance is met.

Ex-Car

We got rid of our old car and immediately regretted our decision. It wasn't that our new car was unsatisfactory; in fact it ran more smoothly and reliably than the old one ever had, even when it was new. But the old car had acquired a "personality" assembled from memories of our lives during the time we owned it, and we found that we missed it deeply, as we would have a favorite cousin who had died or moved away.

A few months after selling the car, we saw it in the parking lot of a restaurant in a nearby town. Our initial reaction was to deny that it was our old car, as the restaurant was of a decidedly inferior quality and, obviously, a place our car would never go. But this car was dented in the same place as our ex-car, and two of the six letters of its chrome nameplate were broken off as they had been on ours, and so there could be no doubt.

We pulled into the restaurant parking lot and looked at our ex-car in the glow of our new car's headlights. Clearly it was sad. Its grille, which, when we owned the car, had the appearance of a wide grin, now resembled a set of teeth gritted in desperate endurance. Its round headlights, once a sign of the car's good nature and eagerness to run, now seemed to indicate shocked surprise. And a crack in the windshield the car used to wear with embattled pride had become a grisly scar, a symbol of our betrayal.

In the end, we had to go into the restaurant and ask the car's new owner if we could buy it back. He thought it over while he chewed on a fish stick, then told us we could have it back for twice the price he bought it for.

We gave the offer serious consideration, but ultimately decided to reject it. On the way across the parking lot I opened up the hatchback of our ex-car and stole the jack. I don't know why I did this; it certainly wasn't in the best interests of our ex-car; but I still have the jack and have not seen the old car again.

Almost

Looking one early morning out the third-floor window of our hotel room during a trip to the city, I saw a man and woman passing, one going east and the other west, on opposite sides of the street. The man, spotting the woman, glanced about the empty sidewalks then reached into his pocket and pulled out a knife. He stepped off the curb and cut a diagonal path between parked cars toward the woman, now walking with her back to him.

Before I could call out to warn her, another man opened an apartment door across the street, startling the knife-wielding man. The new man picked up a newspaper from his stoop, waved to the man with the knife and ducked back inside. The first man hurriedly stowed the knife and resumed walking in his original direction.

Since then I have not gone out onto the street without wondering when, and how often, I am sized up and rejected, for whatever reason, as the object of a violent assault. Perhaps this paranoia would have been mitigated somewhat had I called the police on that day, but I doubted city police would have reacted with appreciation to a report of a crime almost, but not quite, committed.

Treasure

A local legend had it that Indian treasure was buried somewhere in our region, and as boys my friends and I determined that this treasure must lie in a certain triangle of woods bounded by the creek that ran behind our houses, the fence that demarcated the edge of our school's property, and the parking lot of the nearby grocery store. Though young, we were aware that our selection of this particular woods was purely arbitrary and opportunistic, and were skeptical about the likelihood of the local tribes having socked away the kind of treasure—gold, jewels, Spanish doubloons—that we were looking for. Nonetheless, we established a detailed hierarchy of military-style rank for everyone in our group, and organized elaborate searching parties, for which we fashioned special tools and uniforms. For much of one year, we spent every weekend in the woods looking for the treasure, and though it didn't turn up, we made many worthwhile discoveries (of discarded toys, clothing and bottles) that more than justified our efforts.

Our group had a self-proclaimed ringleader, S., an unusually tall, unhandsome boy whom few of us liked but to whose natural leadership abilities we automatically deferred. One fall Saturday, S. shouted to us from his corner of the woods that he had found the Indian treasure. We rushed to the scene to find S. standing over a wooden shoe-shine box, emptied of its usual contents and filled with prosaic household items tightly wrapped in aluminum foil. These included a toothbrush, a roll of tape and a few wooden nickels, which S. had "engraved" with the crude likeness of an Indian princess. He declared that the search was over and that, as the High Commander of the Seekers of the Treasure, the box and its contents belonged to him.

Nobody cared about the fake treasure, though each of us examined it with some interest, hoping to find some shred of evidence that it was real. What most chagrined us, however, was that S.'s cheap ploy had ended our game. The game had depended on an unattainable goal, and now that the goal had been attained, the organization had no reason to exist. Though it would have been possible to call S.'s bluff and expose the treasure as bogus, none of us had either the courage or the heart to do so.

The group soon disbanded, and each of us went our separate ways. Occasionally S. would collar one of us in the halls of our school and insist he had heard about a new treasure, this one in another local woods, but these claims fell upon deaf ears. He had overestimated our loyalty to him as leader, and allowed his pride to topple him. Soon his family would move away to another state, and the members of our group would grow apart, finding new interests and cliques, and the entire treasure-hunting episode would come to seem childish and stupid.

The Bureau

Two couples we knew went together to an estate auction, hoping to find some inexpensive antique furniture. One couple found nothing of interest, but the second couple fell for an old bureau with four drawers and curved inlays, which they agreed would, once refinished, look good in their bedroom. This second couple agreed on a maximum price they would pay, and were thrilled, after a brief run of lackluster bidding, to secure the bureau for much less.

After the auction, the second couple collected their bureau, and the first couple helped them load it into their van. But while they were loading it one of the drawers slid out onto the ground. The husband of the first couple bent to pick up the drawer, and, noticing that it was lined with an old scrap of newspaper, paused to read what was printed there. He was astonished to find that the newspaper was dated just a few days after his own birthday several decades before. Even more astonishing, however, was the fact that the newspaper was from his own home town, many hundreds of miles from here, and that the particular page the drawer was lined with bore the announcement of his own birth. The man's wife and their friends paused to discuss the coincidence for a while, and the man was given the newspaper page and brought it home as a keepsake.

The fact was, the man's parents had been killed in a train accident when he was a baby and he knew very little about their lives. Soon he grew obsessed with the bureau and, convinced it held the key to his buried past, plotted ways to get into the second couple's bedroom to see it. He began stopping by their house on his lunch hour, and struck up a secret friendship with the wife of the second couple, who stayed home during the day to care for her baby. Their friendship developed into a romantic affair, and most days, after they made love and the woman fell asleep, the man would examine the bureau in minute detail, opening and closing the drawers and touching the woodwork with trembling hands.

Eventually the man and woman left their families, married one another, and moved very far away. It wasn't until they arrived in their new town that the man realized the bureau had not come with them. The woman had left it with her ex-husband, who was the one who had liked it in the first place. At first the man was heartbroken, but since there was nothing he could do he gave up thinking about it and concentrated on his new life, which was neither better nor worse than the one he had left behind.

The Cement Mailbox

A farmer who lives on our road had lost three mailboxes in as many weeks to the drunken antics of some local youths, who had taken to driving past late at night and smashing the mailboxes with a baseball bat. Because the police had been uncooperative in apprehending the youths, the farmer devised a solution to the problem: he bought two mailboxes— a gigantic, industrial-strength one and a small aluminum one—and arranged the boxes one inside the other, with a layer of cement between the two. He mounted this monstrous megabox on a length of eight-inch steel pipe, which was set into a four-foot post hole and stabilized there with thirty additional gallons of cement.

The following weekend the youths sped past in their convertible, and T., the captain of the high school baseball team and a local slugger of some renown, swung at the box from a standing position in the back seat. With the bat moving at more than seventy-five miles per hour relative to the car, and the car itself traveling nearly as fast, the combined velocity of the impact was approximately 150 miles per hour. It was at this speed that the bat ricocheted and struck the head of J., a seventeen-year-old girl who had been sitting in the car, killing her instantly.

A series of criminal charges and civil suits followed. T. was tried as an adult and convicted of involuntary manslaughter. The driver of the car was sentenced to community service on charges of vandalism and reckless endangerment.

The farmer was also convicted of reckless endangerment and fined; in response he sued the police department for failing to address the problem beforehand. The parents of the dead girl lobbied to have all the car's living occupants, five in all, expelled from school; they also sued T., the driver and the farmer for several million dollars. They even tried, and failed, to sue the hardware store where the farmer had bought his cement-mailbox supplies, arguing that the store's employees ought to have figured out what the farmer was doing, and stopped him. In a peripheral case, T.'s parents sued the hospital where he was treated for a broken arm; apparently the doctors there had set the break improperly, resulting in a painful re-setting that was likely to ruin T.'s chances to play baseball in the major leagues. Their lawyers demanded a percentage of T.'s projected future salary.

In the end, all judgments were reversed on appeal. It seemed that everyone involved was to blame, which the courts determined was no different from no one being to blame. All that remains, apart from the many legal debts incurred by the litigants and the accused, is the cement mailbox, which has proven too costly and cumbersome to remove.

Trust Jesus

A local teenager was caught spray-painting on an abandoned railroad bridge above a busy two-lane highway. Her graffito, which had nearly been finished when she was apprehended, read: TRUST JESUS.

When her case came before our judge, he asked the teenager why she had done what she did. She apologized, telling him that she "thought it would help." When he asked what it would help, the teenager had no answer, and only reiterated her original statement.

The judge levied a five-hundred-dollar fine and sentenced the girl to repaint the entire bridge, even the portions she had not defaced. Those who suggested to the judge that this was an extreme punishment were met with angry stares.

For some weeks after the ruling, the girl could be seen suspended on a platform above the road after school, painstakingly erasing her original handiwork. She has become something of a local hero and is said to be considering a run for a seat on the town council. Meanwhile, the repainted bridge has become a prime target of vandals, and is now covered with vulgarisms and rude slogans.

Kevin

While eating lunch at a restaurant in the city, I paused to visit the men's room. I like to wear loose-fitting, comfortable pants, and I had discovered that, when I pushed them down to use the toilet, my wallet often slipped out onto the floor. Consequently I developed the habit of removing the wallet from my pocket before I sat down and resting it on the edge of the sink, to protect it from contact with filth. On this particular occasion, since the sink was out of reach of the toilet, I set the wallet on a child's high chair the management had stored in a nearby corner. When I was through I pulled up my pants, washed my hands and departed, leaving the wallet behind.

Ten minutes later I finished eating and offered to buy my companion, an old friend, his meal. It was then that I discovered my wallet was missing. Immediately I remembered where I had left it and went to the men's room to retrieve it. But by now the wallet was gone.

My friend, a keen observer of men, provided an enticing clue. Only one person had entered the men's room after me, and he had been carrying a hammer. Armed with this evidence, we approached the restaurant's owner and told him that my wallet had been taken by a man carrying a hammer. To our surprise, the owner told us that this man was named Kevin, he was a handyman and had been doing repairs in the kitchen.

When my friend and I insisted that it was Kevin, then, who had my wallet, the owner shook his head. He refused to give us Kevin's last name or address, and maintained that Kevin would never do such a thing. He was honest, the owner told us, and would have turned in the wallet had he found it, but Kevin had done nothing of the sort.

Dejected, I left my friend's phone number, imploring the owner to ask Kevin if he had found any "lost" items in the men's room. The owner promised to do so, but I had little hope, and my sympathetic friend agreed to put me up for the rest of my stay in the city, and lent me enough money to enjoy myself.

Thus resigned, I was shocked when Kevin called me at my friend's apartment that night to report that he had the wallet. He explained that he owned a leather-bound notebook that he carried with him on the job, which he used to jot down his ideas and inspirations. This notebook was identical in appearance to my wallet. Apparently he did the same thing I did in men's rooms to keep the notebook clean. What Kevin found extraordinary was that he had forgotten, on this particular day, to bring his notebook to work, an omission he could not recall ever having made before, and this happened to be the same day he found a wallet that looked just like it, sitting in exactly the place he would have put it, had it been his notebook. He wondered aloud if the wallet/notebook shape had some deeper significance, some mystic connection to the place he had found it in, and if some greater power had forced me to leave the wallet, as a stand-in for his notebook. That said, he agreed to leave the wallet at the restaurant the next morning, and when I went to pick it up I found it at the counter, its contents fully accounted for. I never met Kevin.

In the car home from the city I wondered, in the wake of his cryptic comment, what ideas and inspirations the handyman might be writing down in his notebook, and what might have caused him to forget it while I was in town.

Terrorist

In my second year of high school, I attempted, along with two other boys, to drive mad a fourth boy, L., who was the shyest and most awkward member of our small group of social outcasts. The three of us called ourselves the ITO, or Independent Terrorists' Organization, and tortured L. in a variety of ways, including the mailing of anonymous threats, the vandalizing of his car, the dedication to him of hit songs on the local FM radio station, and all manner of obscene and disruptive telephone calls. We invited him to meet us in the middle of a park, arrived early, deposited at the meeting place a cardboard box containing a cow's heart with his name seared into it with a soldering iron, then hid in some nearby trees and took surveillance photos of the event, which photos we subsequently mailed him; we set afire in his yard a small but extremely detailed effigy of him that we had constructed from chicken wire and papier-mâché and soaked in kerosene; we issued an invitation to a nonexistent formal party at the home of a girl he secretly loved, which he dutifully attended, carrying a bouquet; we placed an order at the drive-up window of the fast food restaurant where he worked and came to the pick-up window in a borrowed car, wearing plastic Richard Nixon masks. Though our true identities could never have been far from his discovery, he never accused us, as we three were his best, if not only, friends; and in fact he confided his anxieties to us, and we dutifully promised to help him identify his torturers and punish them in some way once they were unmasked.

This went on for about four months, and ended at my request. In the space of those months, my braces had been taken off, and I was prescribed contact lenses and began dating a girl; and it was in imagining how to explain my behavior to her that I realized how awful that behavior was, and I begged my friends to come clean.

In retrospect, I see that this desire was purely self-serving, and that identifying ourselves was the cruelest trick of all, for there could be no deeper blow for L. than to be confronted with our betrayal, and with the knowledge that, if he reacted appropriately—that is, with anger—he would have no friends left. When we finally revealed ourselves, it was by telegram, and we made sure we were all at his house when it arrived.

His response convinced me that I was a coward, a conviction I still hold to this day. He unfolded the yellow paper, read it aloud, and then laughed as long and as hard as we did.

Directions

The daughter of old friends had decided to attend college in our town, and was to visit the campus with her boyfriend, a pre-med student at a university in another part of the state. As a favor to her parents, we agreed to provide the two with dinner when they arrived, and answer any questions the young woman might have about life in the area. We had not seen her since she was a little girl.

We prepared a lavish meal, eager to help our friends' daughter, and to ease any fears she might have about her new independence.

To our surprise, the couple arrived nearly an hour early, and in a strange condition. They were dressed with extreme informality, their T-shirts soiled and blue jeans stained and torn. Both were personally unkempt, their hair knotted and oily, and they reeked of cigarette smoke. The pre-med student had a pinched, impoverished look about him, as if he had been awake studying for days on end with only coffee to nourish him. Most alarming was the fact that our friends' daughter appeared to be at least seven months pregnant.

Despite our shock, we struggled to make a go of the evening. The couple were obviously hungry, so in lieu of the unfinished meal we made them cold sandwiches, which they ate in huge, anxious bites. We told our friends' daughter about life at the college, which information she received silently, occasionally nodding to indicate she understood. Meanwhile her boyfriend's eyes wandered around the room, as if our modest possessions were priceless items in a museum. At one point they asked if we had anything to drink, and they polished off two brimming glasses of milk each, allowing it to spill over their faces and onto their clothes.

Not much later they rose to leave, so we wished them luck and told them they should feel free to come by anytime. In response, they asked us for directions to a free medical clinic downtown, which we gave them. They thanked us quietly and drove away in a dilapidated Buick that emitted blue smoke.

For some minutes we considered what we would say to our friends, particularly on the subject of the pregnancy, about which they had not warned us. It was during this discussion that a knock came at the door. We opened it to find the real daughter and boyfriend, dressed, respectively, in a yellow designer sundress and a shirt and tie. They apologized for being late and presented us with a bottle of sparkling cider and a plastic container of cupcakes. The daughter kissed our cheeks and the boyfriend shook our hands.

We told them our oven had broken down and took them out to a restaurant. Both talked incessantly and with smug confidence about the careers they had plotted for themselves and the country estate where they planned to live when they graduated. My wife and I found them extremely annoying.

For months afterward we expected, even hoped, to be visited again by the first couple, but they never came back.

Distance

A witness to a prominent local murder fell under close scrutiny during the trial, when it was revealed that, directly after the killing, he had wandered around aimlessly for an hour and a half before reporting the crime to a policeman who happened to be walking by. Asked for an explanation for his behavior, the witness explained that he had been sitting high in the bleachers of the empty football stadium where the murder had taken place, and had seen the shooting, which occurred beneath the goalposts at the opposite end of the field, from a great distance. Though his view of the murder was clear and the sound of the shot quite loud, the witness found it difficult to believe in something that had happened so far away. Upon further questioning, the witness confessed that, had he not encountered the policeman by chance, he might never have reported the crime at all.

When the trial was over, members of the jury expressed their disgust with the witness, whom they characterized as irresponsible at best, and at worst guilty of some sort of crime himself. The foreman, who had been sitting closest to the witness during the trial, even confessed to a desire to physically harm him, and said that he would have done so had the two not been separated by the walls of the jury box and witness stand.

4. Work and Money

In the pocket of a pair of long-forgotten pants I was preparing for donation to Goodwill, I found a ten-dollar bill. This pleased me until I realized that the bill was worth far less than when I put it into my pocket, many years ago. As a gift to my future self, and in a bet against inflation, I added a second ten-dollar bill to the pocket, and replaced the pants in the back of my closet.

Sixty Dollars

All the money I ever found, I found during the same year, in the same town, at exactly the time I most needed it, when I had little income and few prospects for more. I was working part-time at a supermarket and living in a large house with four other recent college graduates, where we subsisted primarily on pasta and beans and cheap beer, and I had begun to pine for a better life, free from incessant worry about my expenses, which at the time included a large credit card debt and a substantial student loan.

The first time I found money, I was walking over a bridge and stopped to gaze down on the river below. After doing so, I happened to look at my feet and noticed that I was standing on a twenty-dollar bill.

The second time, I went into a bank to withdraw twenty dollars from my savings account and saw a twenty-dollar bill lying on the floor. Since the bank had just opened and no other customers were around, I kept it.

The third time, I checked a book out of the library and found twenty dollars pressed between the pages.

Though the sixty dollars might have had the power to change my life—I could have quit my dead-end clerk's job and found something worthwhile—I squandered each of the twenty-dollar bills on expensive restaurant meals. In fact, all three of the meals came out to more than twenty dollars, so I ended up spending money of my own that I would otherwise have saved. I seemed to believe that since the money had been found, not earned, it would somehow be taken from me if I didn't spend it fast. But the result was that I developed a taste for good food and drink, and my near-poverty became all the more difficult to bear.

I now recognize this year as a turning point, but whether it was for the better or the worse remains unclear.

The Pork Chop

My father managed apartment buildings for a living, and every June, when the university students left town, he went through each vacated apartment to clean and repair it for the coming school year. Often he found items left behind: radios, shower supplies, an electric typewriter with the price tag still on it. These things would be given to my sister and me, or, in the years after we moved out of the house, sold at an annual yard sale.

Among the tasks on my father's list was to defrost and wipe clean the refrigerators and freezers. In those days, most freezers tended to accumulate furry mounds of rock-hard ice, which had to melt before my father could complete the job. Consequently, he would spend one day removing all the moldy food, and then the next cleaning the kitchens and their defrosted refrigerators.

Entering an apartment one cleaning day, my father was overwhelmed by a terrible odor. He reasoned that it could not be coming from the refrigerator, as he had purged it of food the day before, so he searched elsewhere—under the oven, inside the cabinets, down the heating ducts—for the dead mouse or squirrel he figured was the source of the smell. Eventually, doubting his memory, he checked the refrigerator once more, and that is when he found the pork chop.

It had been sitting in a plastic bag, sealed into a ridge of freezer ice. Now, to my father's astonishment, it was crawling with maggots. He couldn't understand how the maggots had gotten into the bag so quickly, but there was little time for contemplation: the odor was intensifying. He removed the plastic bag and dropped it into another bag, which he wrapped, double-knotted, in still a third bag. He threw this bag into the dumpster.

Inside the apartment, the smell would not diminish. He lit candles, placed air fresheners everywhere. When he got home, the smell was on his clothes. My mother washed them, but they contaminated the rest of the load. My father showered and brought the smell into the bathroom, where it lingered for weeks. He drove the ruined laundry to the dump and the smell adhered to the trunk of the car, and then leaked into the passenger compartment. Months later, despite my mother's ministrations, the smell could still be discerned in their house. Meanwhile, the apartment was professionally cleaned, twice, with bleach, yet my father still could not rent it for the new school year. The following fall, he was only able to rent it to a woman with a severe cold, who complained incessantly once she recovered, and moved out before the semester was over.

My father, always stoic, rarely mentioned the incident. But my mother talked incoherently about the pork chop on her deathbed. She called me by my father's name and begged me to take it away, to get it out of her hospital room. Not wishing to disobey, yet reluctant to explain the truth, I pretended to toss something into the trash, then moved the metal can into the hallway. After that, however, and up to the moment my mother died, I thought I was able to smell the pork chop myself.

Tool

Though many have expressed doubts about the wisdom of our society's dependence on computer technology, our acquaintance, a computer programmer, was always quick to defend the machines that had made his career possible. Technology, he would say, was never of unambiguous value; every negative effect a new technology precipitated was balanced by some positive change. Computers might not be the answer to every problem, he admitted, but they were certainly the solution to some.

Nevertheless, he suffered a crisis of faith at the height of his career. Computers, he realized, had taken their toll upon him: he suffered from acute back problems, severe eyestrain and poor nutrition, and he had alienated himself from his wife and children with his frequent all-night sessions of programming and Internet use. He decided to take a month's leave from his job to engage in some unmediated personal experience. With his family, he hiked and camped; he studied the lives of birds and plants and learned their names. He took up jogging, and bought himself a workbench and a set of tools.

It was the tools, one tool in particular, that would prove our acquaintance's undoing. In the last week or so of his vacation, he began knocking together some crude wooden items: a toy chest for his son, a stool for his daughter, a coat rack. Especially satisfying to him was the hammer. Though he enjoyed measuring and marking boards, or sawing them to the right length, no activity proved more stimulating than fastening the boards together with his hammer. After a day of hammering, he would lie awake in bed, his mind racing with the shape of the hammer, the sound it made, the sensation of pounding nails into wood with it. In a few days he was coming to bed later and later, and his basement workshop soon filled up with ugly wooden items, many of them of no practical value, nor of any resemblance to recognizable objects. Indeed, he was gripped by a kind of madness, an addiction. When it was time to return to work, he called in sick, and against the objections of his family locked himself in the basement with his beloved tool.

Inevitably, the time came when our acquaintance had to choose between the hammer and the computer. The choice ought to have been obvious: with the computer, he could make a living which would support some abbreviated version of his carpentry habit. But if he chose the hammer he would lose everything.

In the end, the very nature of the tools in question seemed to force his hand. In a fit of despair over his indecision, he used the hammer to destroy his computer.

Since then, his hammer has not done him much additional good; his family is straining to make ends meet with the meager income provided by the woodworking trade, a trade for which he has little natural aptitude and the market for which, in our lively rural milieu, is glutted with skillful practitioners. But when asked if he regrets his decision, he replies that he does not. He stands by his hammer, which he holds up against the computer as a sturdier and more enduring, and thus, in his opinion, superior, technology.

Last Meal

Our many trips to a local diner have resulted in our acquaintance with its short-order cook, a man in his late thirties whose intensive self-training and obsessive attention to detail have resulted in an uncanny ability to make, from such rudiments as eggs, potatoes, meatloaf and cold cuts, rough-hewn delicacies of surprising originality and variety. So pleased does he seem while at work, and so satisfied with his creations, that we were once given to ask if he'd ever made a meal he didn't like.

After some thought, he told us that he had once been employed as the head chef at a state prison, where one night he was asked to cook a last meal for a murderer who had been condemned to death. The murderer had requested a porterhouse steak, medium rare; french fries; a bowl of raspberry sherbet; and a glass of iced tea. As per state prison regulations, it was also required that he be served a green salad. The prisoner was to be executed at midnight and would be served dinner at 7:30 p.m., after the other inmates were through eating.

Though he had little sympathy for the murderer, the cook was opposed to capital punishment and decided to make the meal a special one. He chose an excellent cut of meat and prepared it with a thick, hearty mushroom gravy; he seasoned the fries lightly with paprika and garlic powder and made the sherbet by hand, with real fruit, in an ice-cream maker he brought from home. The iced tea he brewed several hours in the sun, using the finest first-flush Darjeeling he could find, and he garnished it with lemon and a sprig of mint. The salad contained no fewer than six fresh, flavorful greens.

Unfortunately, the meal was returned to the kitchen barely touched, the meat gone cold and tough, the sherbet melted and the fries congealed and pasty. The cook was devastated. It was bad enough, he told us, that he had made an unpalatable meal, but far worse that he had, in the process, ruined a condemned man's final hours.

My wife and I immediately pointed out that the meal might well have been wonderful, but the man's life was about to end, and he was likely too lost in thoughts of death to eat. The cook said that this was nice of us to suggest, but he knew the truth, and would regret that meal for the rest of his life.

Since then we have always, after eating at the diner, commented generously on the high quality of our food.

Too Well

A man we know, whose friends are few and not especially close, works as an inspector of industrial machinery, a job that involves much travel and which rarely brings him into contact with others. Among the tools of his trade is a voice-activated tape recorder, with which he records his comments and recommendations about the machinery he inspects. The tapes are transcribed by a secretary he rarely sees and the transcriptions returned to him for editing into a formal report.

One particularly hectic week, our acquaintance lost his tape recorder, along with the tape inside, which held his notes from a recent inspection. After several days of searching, he was forced to buy a new recorder and schedule another inspection of the same factory.

A few days before he was to reinspect the factory, he found his old recorder: it had fallen into the plastic cubbyhole on the driver's-side door of his car, and been hidden there by a folded map. Relieved, he sent the tape to his secretary and canceled the new appointment.

Soon he received the transcription of the missing tape. His notes, as expected, were intact, but attached to them were several pages of gibberish, which after long consideration he identified as his own thoughts, the ones he'd had during the past week of silent drives to inspection sites. He realized that his tape recorder must have been turned on when he dropped it, and that its voice-activation mechanism had sprung into action each time he spoke in the car. Evidently he had been talking to himself, something he never knew he was doing. Still more surprising was the nature of his spoken thoughts: they were expressions of pure melancholy, of longing, of dread at the prospect of the empty, lonesome days before him. One entire page consisted of the phrase "I have no friends," repeated over and over.

He has since made an effort to strengthen his friendships; indeed, it is this very effort that allowed us to hear his story, as he shared it with us over a dinner he made himself in his immaculate and empty house. Unfortunately, intimacy does not come naturally to our acquaintance, and the evening grew very uncomfortable after the telling of his story, and we went home far earlier than expected. Since then we have tried to think of a woman we could introduce him to, but so far have failed to come up with anyone who might like him. We did suggest that he call his secretary, who after all has heard his voice more than anyone else he knows. But he says that she knows him too well. About this he may be right.

The Expert

A café opened in our town which specialized in unusual gourmet coffees from estates throughout Central and South America, Africa, India and the Pacific Islands. The entrepreneurs who ran the café hired a grizzled adventurer and self-proclaimed coffee expert, whose job was to fly once a year to the oldest and most remote estates, and gather the coffees that would be offered at the café for the rest of the year. The expert was paid handsomely and reimbursed for his considerable expenses, but his work paid off: the café became one of the most popular and lucrative businesses in our town, and the entrepreneurs celebrated their success by reinvesting their profits in more treacherous and far-ranging coffee-research expeditions.

One morning several years into the café's existence, an electrical fire claimed the rear half of the building it occupied. Though the seating area was unharmed, the storeroom was completely consumed, along with all the coffee the expert had just brought back from his journey to Kenya, Guatemala and the Oaxaca region of Mexico. For days, the rich smell of roasting coffee filled the air, and the remaining supply quickly dwindled to the edge of nothing.

The café had reached a crisis, and the entrepreneurs had to take drastic measures. They went out to the supermarket and bought several cases of its store-brand beans, then brought them back, ground them and served them to their regular customers.

The entrepreneurs were surprised to learn that, while the customers noticed the difference, they didn't seem to care. After a few weeks, the owners fired the expert. They explained that while the contrast between the coffees was drastic, and they would miss the delicious blends from all over the world, they preferred to hang on to their money. From then on, they said, they would buy their coffee from the supermarket.

The expert, already known in our town long before the entrepreneurs arrived as a misanthropic crackpot, responded by burning the café entirely to the ground. He was captured with his matches and gas can at the supermarket, which he had planned to torch next.

From prison, he told reporters that the well-documented humiliations and privations of incarceration paled in comparison to jail coffee, which was very nearly the worst he had ever tasted.

The Uniform

In the early days of the Cold War, the United States government spent significant amounts of money testing the effects of nuclear explosions on buildings, roads, cars, trains, household items and, ultimately, living beings. Since no military personnel, of course, were willing to sacrifice their own lives in the tests, a substitute for soldiers had to be found, and the government soon settled on pigs for this purpose.

To make the tests as authentic as possible, Army scientists ordered that military uniforms be fitted to the pigs, and a local company was contracted to do this. It happened that the company was owned by my future father-in-law, a retired Army officer who had fought in the war and had dedicated his civilian life to textile manufacture, the family business. The project was secret, and the uniforms were to be made in pieces by employees working alone. The pieces would be assembled by my father-in-law personally, and no one else was to see the finished product.

My father-in-law, however, found the completed uniforms to be quite sharp, and got the idea that one would look good on his beloved pet, a German shepherd named Ace. He particularly liked a certain detail of the uniforms—an embroidered name patch with the word PIG stitched onto it—because among Ace's distinguishing characteristics was a tendency to eat messily and in haste. He ordered his employees to make enough material for a couple of extra uniforms, which he sewed together at home, tailoring them perfectly to Ace's measurements. Whenever the two went out, Ace wore his Army uniform, and occasionally my father-in-law would pin a few of his own medals onto the dog's chest, if the dog had been especially obedient or kind on that day.

It wasn't long before an active officer from the base saw my father-in-law and Ace in a bar together, and when they returned home they found two military police awaiting them. The MPs confiscated the uniform and my father-in-law was reprimanded severely; in addition he was subjected to a harsh grilling and forced to provide a list of everyone in town who might have seen the uniform. From then on, whenever he was seen in town with Ace, the dog wore nothing but his collar.

Years later, when my wife's parents moved closer to our area, my father-in-law brought the duplicate uniform with him. Since Ace's death he has had several dogs, all German shepherds of Ace's approximate size, all of whom he named Ace and who have all, on occasion, worn the forbidden uniform.

Recently he and the latest Ace met a retired Army officer who was once stationed at the base where the nuclear testing was to have taken place. My father-in-law boldly told him where the dog's uniform had come from. To everyone's surprise, the officer remembered my father-in-law, and told him that he had, in the old days, been regarded as a suspected spy. The officer further admitted that there had been a thick file at the base with his name on it.

Immediately my father-in-law set out to get a copy of this file, and after much wrangling and red tape, acquired it through the Freedom of Information Act. It contains dozens of black-and-white surveillance photos of him and Ace, a few of my wife's mother and several of long-forgotten house-guests; there are also hundreds of pages of descriptions of their mundane domestic activities, and the addresses and telephone numbers of all their old friends. The file and uniform are my father-in-law's favorite conversation pieces, and he proudly brings them out whenever he has visitors.

Master

Our friend recently left his job as system operator for a local Internet service provider. Since he was known as a computer expert, and loved his work, we were surprised to learn he had quit, and so one evening had him over for dinner to find out what had happened.

He told us this story: late one night he was awakened by an alarm he had rigged on his own computer, to alert him of problems with the ISP's servers. His computer told him that the system was refusing subscribers, so he dressed and went in to the office to see what was the matter. There he discovered that the system had crashed. He worked all night and well into the next day to alleviate the problem, which proved to have originated with a software bug.

Exhausted from the hours of effort, he brought the system back on line, only to find that something terrible had happened: the e-mail that had been stored in subscribers' accounts over the past twenty hours had somehow been erased. Retracing his steps, our friend found that the mistake this time had been his own; he had inadvertently cleared all stored mail when he reset the network.

Since he knew that customers depended heavily on their e-mail, he decided to send a message to all subscribers, alerting them that twenty hours of mail had been lost, and apologizing for the inconvenience. But when his employer caught wind of this plan, she stopped him. Mistakes like this happen, she reasoned; nobody would even notice, and those who did would resolve the problem on their own. Sending a message admitting the error would cause more harm than good.

Our friend was tired and upset, and wearily came around to his boss's way of thinking. But that night, unable to sleep, he put together a search program that would, over the next week, examine—for certain key words and phrases indicating jealousy, anger, remorse, or accusation resulting from the loss of important messages—every e-mail that passed through the network. This was strictly illegal, but a negative result would put our friend's mind at ease, and he figured nobody would ever know.

About that, he was correct. But the results of the search were far from negative. Dozens of e-correspondents, he discovered, had suffered catastrophic fallout from the lost messages, including the break-up of romances and friendships, the termination of jobs and, in one case, ill health resulting from missing medical advice. Mortified, our friend began an intensive campaign of reconciliation, sending anonymous flowers and gifts and apologizing profusely under assumed names. But it was all to no avail. The damage had been done and could not be reversed.

After dinner, our friend burst into tears. He told us that he had some money saved up, but jobs were at a premium in our area and he had little hope of holding out long enough to find one he was qualified for. We suggested that he apply for system operator jobs in other towns, but our friend ruefully refused. There should be no system operators, he said. What single mailman served so many thousands, or delivered in such volume? Such responsibility, he believed, should be shared by many, for any compassionate person would crack under its strain. He begged us to cancel our own Internet subscription and return to written correspondence and actual, as opposed to virtual, commerce. Our need would drive our system operator mad.

I am embarrassed to admit that our Internet and e-mail usage has not changed. We still see our friend, but he remains unemployed.

Money Isn't Everything

Thanks to an investment that he described as purely unpremeditated, the result of an overheard conversation in a fast food restaurant, a man we knew struck it rich on the stock market, and then, years later, on the very eve of the market's collapse, sold everything, an act he insisted was impulsive, and due to no particular knowledge on his part. Soon after making these fortuitous decisions, the now-rich man got married and moved into a beautiful new house. His life, by all accounts, was one of ease and satisfaction.

Rumors spread, however, that this happiness was short-lived. When we saw the man on the street, he explained. His wife had found another man, he told us. In addition, his dog had died, his favorite sports team had fallen upon hard times, and the political situation filled him with despair.

Wasn't it true, we asked him, that the real cause of his unhappiness was that he felt trapped by his affluence, which he knew, deep down, that he didn't really deserve?

Oh, no, he explained—if it weren't for his wealth, he would probably be even more unhappy.

But didn't he have to admit that, ultimately, his money had done nothing to enhance his life, and had created unrealistic expectations for his future happiness?

Not at all, he said—his money had greatly improved his lot, and he went to sleep every night thanking his lucky stars it had come his way.

Though we parted that day on excellent terms, we have not attempted to contact the man since. It would be difficult to socialize with someone too stubborn to admit that money isn't everything.

5. Parents and Children

When my wife was pregnant with each of our children, I imagined clearly their future appearance and demeanor. It was young men that I imagined, but my wife gave birth to daughters. Today, when I see my grown daughters, I often have the strong but incorrect impression that I have someone I would like them to meet, and realize that it is the imaginary men I thought they might become to whom I want to introduce them, and with whom I believe they would really hit it off.

Lost

When I was two, I wandered away. My mother was washing dishes in the kitchen and watching me through the window, and in the glare of the setting sun mistook a bucket upturned on a mound in the sandbox for my body, hunched over in concentration. When the telephone rang and the police said they had me, my mother laughed and told them I was home, playing in the sandbox. She had to go out into the yard herself before she would believe them.

No harm had come to me, and apparently I didn't cry. But the pedestrian mall where the police found me was a dozen blocks from our house, and by my mother's reckoning I could not have been gone more than ten minutes. I was able to walk, of course, but not so quickly nor with such purpose and determination. So how did I get there?

In the car on the way home, my mother asked me that very question, and I am said to have answered, *Somebody.* I would not elaborate and giggled when pressed. This does not sound like me, of course, but what do I know? My imagination, my sense of humor, my willingness to reveal myself: these things could not have been then exactly as they are today, and I have no reason to doubt my mother's memory.

The point of this story used to be the mystery of my kidnapper. Now, however, I see it another way. Until I disappeared, my mother had either accompanied me at all times, or left me with my father, or a neighbor or babysitter, someone who could account for the time with me she'd missed;

she could know what I'd done and seen and said, and where I'd been. But she could not know the make of the car I was conveyed in that day, nor the shape of the person who'd taken me, nor the names of the people who passed me and wondered whose child I was and what I was doing alone. My life had diverged completely from hers for the first time.

As for me, I don't remember the incident at all. Those days have always been lost to me.

Wake

The old man died, and our friend, his daughter, invited us to the wake. On the phone, she told us the circumstances of his death: he'd had a heart condition, and had been prescribed pills in a large green bottle which he was to take three times daily. The prescription could be refilled at any time, indefinitely, and the old man had plenty of money, but a habit of tight-fistedness drove him to short his dosage, presumably to conserve the precious pills. Consequently, he suffered a stroke and died on the way to the hospital.

It so happened that the old man was a connoisseur, and had, over the years, amassed a large collection of fine and extravagant goods: wines and liqueurs and rare single-malt Scotches, obscure and expensive pipe tobacco, black-market cigars. Many of his acquaintances, however, never knew he possessed these things, because the old man would always smoke cheap cigarettes and drink the most pedestrian of drinks out of colorful metal cans.

Not surprisingly, his many children loathed their father's miserly ways and spent their adulthoods compensating with unbridled hedonism, which aged them prematurely and generated crushing debt. Though our friend did not mention it, the old man's will was said to have erased their debts instantly, with enough left over to keep them in cars, hotels, sumptuous meals and new clothes for more than a year. The will had also provided for a huge wake, at which the children and their guests were supposed to consume every last precious item in the cellar. It was to this wake that our friend invited us.

It was a memorable party, to say the least. The hundreds of guests drank themselves into a stupor, and a thick, aromatic smoke filled the air until dawn. Everyone had a wonderful time. Our friend, however, could be seen dashing from room to room in a kind of fury, her face red and her hair streaming out behind her as if in a strong wind. At one point we stopped her and asked why she seemed so angry.

She replied that the old man had ruined her enjoyment by martyring himself: all she could think of was his privation, and how he had sacrificed his own pleasure to augment his friends'. At this point we suggested that perhaps her father had in fact taken great pleasure in the anticipation of satisfaction, more than he might have taken in the satisfaction itself, and we noted that he probably imagined this party with great joy, as much joy as the guests were feeling at that moment, if not more.

This gave our hostess pause, but it was only a few seconds before she shook her head and told us that she didn't know what we were talking about. She stalked off, angrier than ever.

We fell asleep during the cab ride home, and nothing has tasted as good to us since.

Expecting

A local young man, still in high school, announced to his parents that his girlfriend was pregnant and that they intended to marry. His father, eager for his only child to attend a reputable university and major in genetic engineering, which field the father rightly believed held great potential for wealth and fame, grew angry at his son and insisted that the girl have an abortion. He demanded that his son go pick up the girl immediately so that he, the father, could tell her this in person.

The son obeyed, but unwillingly, and his emotional state when he left probably contributed to the terrible automobile accident he became involved in on the way, which killed him.

His girlfriend, in despair over the loss of her lover and reluctant to bring a fatherless child into the world, resolved to have an abortion after all. But when the young man's father got wind of this, he phoned the girl and insisted that she carry the baby to term. The girl refused. The father then bribed the girl's best friend in order to learn where and when the abortion was to take place, and was waiting at the clinic for the girl when she arrived.

According to eyewitnesses, the girl and the older man argued through the window of his car, and then the girl got in and the two argued further, perhaps for as long as thirty minutes. Eventually they pulled away from the clinic.

No one has seen either since, though the father, who we now can refer to as the grandfather, is said to have sent photographs of his grandson to certain acquaintances. It is also rumored that the young man's girlfriend is once again expecting.

The Mothers

Local mothers banded together to exchange advice about and support for the difficult task, which they all shared, of balancing personal ambition and fulfillment with the demands of home and family. Their association was regarded as a great success, and a new sense of confidence and calm seemed to settle over our town, the likes of which had not previously been seen.

So fond of one another did area mothers become that they arranged to take a trip together, an ocean cruise. Area fathers rearranged their work schedules to accommodate the mothers, and prepared to emulate, while they were away, those qualities most commonly associated with the mothers.

While the mothers were gone, our town's business both private and professional stopped entirely, and the streets filled up with fathers and children acting in a manner that encompassed not only fatherliness and childishness but motherliness as well. It was impossible to pin down exactly what behavior, speech or patterns of thought constituted this motherliness, yet all agreed that there was a surrogate motherliness in the air, neither as full nor as satisfying as the real thing, yet a fair substitute nonetheless.

When the mothers returned, their own inherent qualities had intensified, or perhaps it only seemed that way, as we had grown used to their absence. Whatever the case, this motherliness, combined with that which we had developed without them, created an excess, and emotions ran high for several weeks while we regained our equilibrium.

Though no one wishes to deprive the mothers of further associations, we all found this experience unsettling, and have asked them to refrain in the future from departing all at once. To this, the mothers have agreed, though not without some reluctance.

The Fathers

The fathers in our town began to worry that they were paying their children insufficient attention, so a coalition of
concerned fathers arranged a picnic, to be held at our lakeside park, which all the fathers and their children were expected to attend. Those games traditionally played between
fathers and children—baseball and football, for example—
were organized; food, such as hot dogs and hamburgers, that
children most commonly associated with their fathers, was
cooked; and live entertainment determined to be fatherly in
nature—specifically, a rock concert—was scheduled.

Few would argue that the fathers and children did not
have a good time. Nevertheless, things did not go quite as
planned. The children objected to the fathers' participation
in games, as their large size and superior skills upset the balance of play. The food, which the children especially sa-
vored, was refused by many fathers, who, concerned about
their health, wished to avoid cholesterol, carbohydrates, or fat.
And the rock concert, which addressed the generational gap
by including both "oldies" and loud contemporary music,
succeeded at neither, driving the children to the lakeside,
where they threw rocks into the water and at one another,
and pushing the fathers into little groups, where they dis-
cussed sports and drank beer.

When the picnic was over, some suggested that the very
detachment from their children that the fathers displayed

was a defining characteristic of fatherhood, and should be embraced, not discouraged. This suggestion was received with approval by fathers and children alike, and no further picnics are planned.

Sons

A prominent prewar writer, whose novels of manners sold briskly in their time, was notorious for his tumultuous personal life, in which he was said to have driven his wife to suicide and treated his only child, a son, with terrible cruelty. By the time he reached the age of fifty, the writer had stopped writing entirely, and fell into a prosperous but miserable retirement in a village not far from here, shunned by critics and forgotten by his readers.

Meanwhile, his son, who had fallen into delinquency and poor health early in life, recovered his civility during a two-year stay at a home for wayward boys, and began to learn the craft of writing himself. He published a series of angry and shocking novels that revealed, in fictional form, all the transgressions of his father, who consequently was catapulted back into the public consciousness, this time as a monstrous child abuser and wife-beater. The son's novels, unlike his father's, garnered enormous critical praise and countless literary awards, and were certain to endure, sealing his father's ill reputation indefinitely.

In time the son himself had a son, and treated him with the utmost kindness and respect, allowing him all possible advantages and rarely, if ever, reprimanding him for any action regardless of how wayward or ill-mannered, with the intention of ensuring his own reputation as a benevolent parent. However, the child fell in with a bad crowd, and after his own period of incarceration grew up to make a series of well-received films documenting his life with an irrespon-sible and selfish father who lacked the courage to discipline his child.

This turn of events recently drove the critically acclaimed writer to suicide. His father, the forgotten writer, is himself still alive and in his late eighties, and we see him from time to time at the supermarket, thumping melons or examining tomatoes for bruises, like any regular old man. He is said to have altered his will so that his estate will be passed on to his grandson.

Different

My father died suddenly, before I had given serious thought to his mortality, let alone my own, and the effect upon me of his passing was a devastating and completely unexpected midlife crisis which, though no different from those experienced by any number of men and women my age, nevertheless convinced me that I was forever and drastically changed, with no hope of return to the confident days of my youth. I looked the same, but felt certain that my body was only a meaningless shell, the contents of which had been drained away.

The day after his funeral, I found myself hungry and sat at the kitchen table eating marinated olives from a disposable plastic tub. After a while I'd had enough of the olives' saltiness and took from a bowl a ripe red plum. The plum had a small plastic sticker attached to it, printed with the product code used by the store, which I peeled off. I looked around for a place to put the sticker, and settled finally on the lid of the olive tub.

At this point I noticed an identical product code sticker on the lid, and remembered that I had done this very thing— followed a snack of olives with a juicy plum—just four days ago, only hours before I learned of my father's death.

My midlife crisis continued for most of that year, but I believe that its severity was considerably lessened by this coincidence.

The Denim Touch

When my oldest daughter was a small child, I invented bed-time stories to lull her to sleep at night. Most of these stories were forgotten immediately, but a few she requested again and again, and to these I would add events and characters, extemporaneously extending them into small epics, the de-tails of which my daughter could recall with fanatic speci-ficity. One such story was called "The Denim Touch."

The good king of a distant country, the story went, had a single daughter, whom he loved with all his heart. One day a prince came to ask for the daughter's hand. To win the good king's favor, the prince gave him a magical candlestick that, if rubbed in conjunction with a strange incantation, would enable its bearer to turn anything he wished into denim. The king accepted the gift and gave his blessing for their marriage. But at the wedding, the king danced with his daughter and, under the candlestick's power, inadvertently turned her into denim. The heartbroken prince took up his denimed bride and from then on roamed the countryside, wearing her like a suit, mourning her tragic transformation. The story then became episodic, as the prince sought some way to restore the princess to her original form.

For years I produced installments of "The Denim Touch" for my daughter. Then, one night, she asked me a startling question: where did the princess go? It happened that earlier this particular week our family had lost a beloved dog to old age and buried him in the woods near our home.

I reminded her that the princess had turned to denim, and the prince was trying to turn her back. Yes, I know, my daughter said, but where *is* she? He is wearing her, I explained. Yes, my daughter said, but *where is she?*

Perhaps because it was late, perhaps because I was still emotionally exhausted from the death of my dog, I confessed that I didn't know. She was just nowhere, I supposed.

This threw my daughter into paroxysms of grief, and for the first time I was given to wonder why I had told her such a macabre story in the first place, or why such a story would even enter my head. Consumed with guilt, I apologized profusely, and blurted a final installment of the story, in which the princess is cured by a good witch and the couple become king and queen of all the land. Unfortunately, this was no longer sufficient, and from then on I read bedtime stories out of books.

Even now, however, I find myself lying awake on restless nights, devising new installments of "The Denim Touch." I wouldn't dare tell them to my children, who are grown, or to the children they might someday bear, yet I continue to invent them nonetheless. Perhaps they are a form of prayer: there is considerable comfort in this endless tale of impending resurrection, and since I claim no formal religious affiliation, the stories may fill a need I am not fully aware I possess.

Whatever the reason, when my wife reaches out and embraces me during the night, I am reminded of the loyal prince wearing his own wife, and I am able at last to sleep.

Mice

A doctor we know lived, as a little girl, out in the country, in a house on the edge of a forest not far from here. Because of its rural location, and because it was the only one for several miles around, the house developed a mouse infestation, and our friend's family often found their stored food broken into and eaten.

Our friend's father bought a number of mousetraps and placed them throughout the house. In time, several mice were caught and killed by the traps, and our friend went with her father to dispose of their bodies in the woods. The father removed them by their tails from a small cardboard box and tossed them out among the trees.

A child of the country, our friend was accustomed to the death of animals and accepted that it was sometimes necessary. Her father hunted deer and game birds, which they ate, and this did not bother her. But for some reason, the capture and disposal of the mice upset her greatly. She decided to trick her father and developed a plan: she would go into the forest and recover the tiny corpses, then bring them home and set them in the traps. This way her father would believe the mice were being eliminated, and she would have the satisfaction of knowing she had saved their lives.

The plan worked well all through the winter, when the dead mice could easily be found on the surface of the snow and their bodies were neatly preserved in the freezing air. But by spring it became necessary to allow new mice to be caught, owing to the difficulty of recovering the corpses, and to the problem of their rapid decomposition. Our friend became distraught: the lives of the mice were solely in her control, and so she had an obligation to continue saving them. But was it all right to allow new mice to be killed, to save the few she could? Or was it her responsibility to develop a better plan, one that would save all the mice? Her problems worsened when she grew ill and was confined to bed for a week. Though her health improved, she cried and cried, and neither her parents nor her doctor could understand why.

In time our friend grew up and she forgot about her plan to save the mice. She went to college and medical school, and became an obstetrician and fertility expert at the county hospital, which is where we first met her. Often, in recent years, she has administered drugs to women who encountered difficulty conceiving children, and these drugs sometimes result in high multiple pregnancies of five, six, seven or more. When this happens she strongly recommends that the patient permit her to abort several of the fetuses, so that the remaining few will be carried safely to term.

One morning she was performing this very procedure on a patient of hers and was overcome, inexplicably, by emotion. She laid down her instruments and stepped back from the table, then asked a young resident to take over. She left the room and sat very still and quiet in her office, and a strange fantasy occurred to her: she would take away the barely developed aborted fetuses, and incubate them and administer the most up-to-date care, and they would grow up like normal children and would be hers to keep, because she had been unable, despite all her knowledge and expertise, to conceive children herself.

It wasn't long, however, before this fantasy struck her as unprofessional at best and sickening at worst, and many months later she successfully delivered her patient's triplets. The patient never learned, and the doctor never told her, that the original procedure had been performed by someone else.

Tea

In the years after my father died, my mother took to a certain brand of tea, which she drank four times daily, once at breakfast, twice in midafternoon and once in the evening, after dinner. She drank it with milk and honey, though sometimes I saw her use granulated sugar, when the honey ran out.

This particular tea came in boxes of fifty bags, and every box came with a small pastel-colored ceramic circus figurine. It was a kind of promotion: I believe the tea was called Piccadilly Circus, and there were fifteen different figurines, a lion tamer, an acrobat, a human cannonball. Every once in a while I would be around when my mother unwrapped a new box and took out the figurine. It would sit on the table between us while we drank and sometimes she would pick it up and turn it over in her hand.

When my mother died and my sister and I sorted through her possessions, we found, in the back of the cellar, a pile of shoeboxes with numbers written on the top: 80, 100, 75. When we opened them we found the figurines. The numbers on top corresponded to the number of figurines inside.

It wasn't like our mother to keep things; she was no pack rat. Because of this it seemed right to take out the figurines and count them, which we did. There were 420. Sitting there in the dusty cellar, I calculated: fifty tea bags times 420 boxes of tea was 21,000 cups. If each cup held about eight ounces of tea, that made 168,000 ounces, which divided by 128 ounces per gallon was more than 1,300 gallons of tea.

In my head I expressed this in fifty-gallon drums, about twenty-five of them, stacked up in a big pyramid, and I pictured them stored out in the wind and cold on a cement lot, in back of an airport or warehouse somewhere, behind a tall chain-link fence.

It occurred to me that this was a measure of loneliness, all the tea my mother drank during the twelve years between my father's death and her own. I wondered if she herself thought of it that way. In any event, when I am lonely, it is the pyramid of fifty-gallon drums that I think of, standing in a light snowstorm, with perhaps a little creamy brown tea leaking from the bottom of one of the drums and frozen into a dull, irregular pattern on the pavement below.

Deaf Child Area

At a bend in a winding country road outside town, there once lived a family whose only child, a girl, was born deaf. When the girl grew old enough to play outside on her own, the family had the county erect a yellow sign near the house which read DEAF CHILD AREA. The idea was that motorists would drive more slowly, knowing that a nearby child could not hear their approach.

By the time I was a boy, the deaf child had become a teenager, and after a while left town for college. She returned occasionally to visit, but for the most part was no longer around. Eventually she married and settled in a faraway city. Her parents, aware of the sign's superfluity, wrote a letter asking the county to come take it down; and though the county promised to see to the matter, no workmen ever arrived.

At about the time I myself married, the deaf child's parents retired and decided to move away to someplace warmer. They sold their house, and it was promptly bought by a local professor. The professor, however, was soon offered a position at another university, which he was obliged to occupy immediately. With no time to sell the house he had just bought, the professor hired a property management company to offer the house for rent. At this point it caught my attention. My wife was pregnant with our first child, and we had begun to worry that our small apartment would be unsuitable for raising a family. After a look at the house in the country, we decided to rent it, and soon moved in.

For several months we ignored the sign, which had grown old and battered, and at any rate had nothing to do with us. But as winter approached and my wife's due date drew near, I noticed that her eyes lingered on the sign whenever we pulled into the driveway, and more than once I caught her staring out at it from our future child's bedroom, which we had furnished and filled with colorful toys. One night, as we lay awake in bed, my wife turned to me and asked if I might remove the sign somehow. She realized she was being irrational, but nonetheless feared the sign might bring some harm to our baby, and she didn't think she could sleep until the sign was gone.

This seemed perfectly reasonable. I got out of bed and dressed, then brought a box of tools out to the roadside, where I examined the sign. I saw that it had been bolted onto a metal post, and that I could simply remove the sign and leave the post where it stood in the ground. I did this quickly, and prepared to go inside.

But something compelled me to go out behind the house and find a shovel, which I used to dig the post out of the ground. The ground was cold, and the work slow going. When I finished, I took the sign and post and put them in the back of the car, and drove down to the lake, where I threw them out as far as I could into the water. They splashed onto the surface and sank out of sight.

When I returned home, my wife didn't ask me where I'd driven. After that we slept comfortably, and did so every night until our child was born without illness or defect.

The Branch

A young man, while hiking, found a crooked branch that had fallen from a dying tree. The branch was nicely balanced, with a fine heft and a stout base that did not sink into the ground as he walked. He held it just above a knot in the wood, and used it to steady himself when he encountered difficult terrain or a steep grade.

When he was through hiking, he paused, considering whether he should toss the branch back into the woods. After some deliberation, he decided to bring it home with him.

One bright afternoon some months later, the young man found the branch and decided to put some additional work into it. He sawed off the cracked shaft above the knot and carved the knot into a handle; then he sanded the entire branch. He hiked with the branch a few more times, then forgot about it. It only crossed his mind when he moved from one apartment to another, and had to pack it with his other belongings.

The young man married and had children, and the children grew to school age. One day they found the branch lying in the attic, and with help from their mother cleaned it up, stained and varnished it, and gave it to their father for his birthday. He was pleased to see that the branch had been so lovingly finished, and for several years used it whenever he went hiking. For a few weeks, after he injured his knee playing touch football, the man used the branch to help him navigate sidewalks and the hallways of his office. When a

143

few co-workers commented on what a nice cane he had, he corrected them, saying that it was simply a walking stick.

After a while, the man grew old, and his knee injury, from which he had never fully recovered, began to give him more trouble. He took to using the branch again. On some days his knee hurt less than on others, but even on these days he carried the walking stick, as it had become a kind of personal trademark, and he would have felt more self-conscious without it than he did with it. People still commented that he had a nice cane and asked him where he had gotten it, and while he was always pleased to tell them the story, he was nonetheless compelled to correct them, saying that it was a walking stick, not a cane.

Then one day the branch slipped on a wet patch of pavement while the old man was getting into his car, and he fell and bruised his hip. On his lunch hour he limped to the hardware store and found a bin filled with rubber caps, and rooted through them until he found one that fit snugly on the base of the branch.

Since then, he has invariably referred to the branch as his cane. We know this man, and can confirm that he corrects people with considerable vehemence whenever they mistakenly call it a walking stick.

Kiss

Our daughter attended a preschool overseen by an attractive, friendly young woman, a professional caregiver who, far from considering her job a burden, seemed to regard the children she supervised with genuine affection, even love. When I dropped my daughter off in the morning, the caregiver welcomed her with open arms, enthusiastically shouting her name; and when I picked her up in the afternoon, she hugged the caregiver and told her she would miss her when they were apart. In addition, I truly liked the caregiver and was always pleased to know that my daughter was with her.

One busy afternoon I arrived flustered and late to pick up my daughter, and after thanking the caregiver for waiting, I kissed her full on the mouth. As if this wasn't enough, I put a firm hand on the small of her back and pulled her close while doing so. It was a fine kiss, sensuous and arousing, but only when I noticed the unfamiliar smell of the caregiver's hair did I realize that, momentarily confused by her obvious regard for my daughter, I had mistaken her for my wife. I released the caregiver, embarrassed, and took my daughter's hand.

To my surprise, the caregiver acted as if nothing unusual had happened. She said bye-bye to my daughter, told me she would see me in the morning, and turned back to her remaining students, who had continued their play oblivious to my gaffe. My daughter, far from confirming my suspicion that she would relate the incident to her mother, also behaved in typical fashion, and showed no signs of emotional distress. My subsequent encounters with the caregiver were cordial, and the kiss was never mentioned again. My only conclusion can be that this sort of thing happens all the time, though when I think about the incident, as I often do, it is generally with enormous guilt and shame.

Coupon

When we thought my mother was dying, my sister and I established a system of shifts in the hospital whereby one of us would be with her at all times, while the other could relax or straighten our mother's affairs, staying within reach, of course, of a telephone. The hospital room itself was gray and bleak, with a television always on and silent nurses moving ominously about, and our mother slipped in and out of consciousness there for several days.

One night my sister fell asleep on her shift, and when she woke, our mother was conscious and lucid and engaged her in conversation. Her surprising recovery was swift, and within a week she was home again. She would live another four years in reasonably good health.

Soon after she was released from the hospital, she told my sister and me that it was because of us that she had returned from the edge. The night before she regained consciousness, she said, she heard us talking to one another in bright, youthful voices, and our optimistic tone had convinced her that she should fight for life. She described our conversation. My sister was said to have greeted me, and I apparently told her she looked wonderful and commented on her clothing, and she then told me about a party she was planning on attending, and I said that I, too, was going to that same party. Our mother attached special significance to the party; she laughed and recalled wanting to attend it too. Aghast, we thanked her for acknowledging us. We didn't tell her the truth, that my sister had been asleep and that I had been at home on the telephone, calling caterers for what we thought would be her funeral.

Some time after my mother did die, I watched a television movie I'd videotaped around the time of her illness. During a commercial break there was an ad for laundry detergent. Two good-looking young people, and man and a woman, engaged in some flirtatious banter at a public laundromat, and I recognized their conversation as the one my mother had attributed to my sister and me on the eve of her recovery.

I promptly wrote a letter to the detergent company, telling them the entire story. Not long afterward I received a coupon good for a free box of detergent. No other reply was provided.

6. Artists and Professors

Our friend, a sculptor, told us that sculpture cannot be taught; rather, it can only be experienced. Similarly, another friend, who is a writer, told us that it is impossible to teach anyone how to write; the writer must learn by doing. Presented with the comments of the other, each insisted that only he himself was correct, the writer stating that sculpture was an elitist and wholly artificial endeavor, whose existence depended solely on its institutional perpetuation, and the sculptor insisting that writing, far from being a true art, was a purely academic exercise. Each man heads the department dedicated to his specific field at our local university.

The Obelisk of Interlaken

Some years ago an article appeared in the newspaper of a village a few miles north of here, claiming that a local farmer had unearthed a large object believed to have originated with a pre-Columbian Indian tribe, or even possibly with the Vikings. The story was generally thought to be improbable, but many of us made the short drive to the village to see for ourselves. Though most came away from the object convinced of its fraudulence, few were disappointed to have seen it. Particularly satisfying was meeting its caretaker, a diminutive, knobbly man of about seventy, who enthusiastically told the story of its discovery beneath his potato patch, and even displayed a piece of metal from his tractor that he claimed the object damaged as he turned it up. The object itself was a four-sided column standing more than twenty-five feet high, the corners converging to a point at the top, which the farmer had marked with a customized brass plaque reading THE OBELISK OF INTERLAKEN.

It did not take long for the obelisk to capture the attention of a pair of academics from our university, an anthropologist and a historian, both renowned for their work at home and abroad, and for their books, considered by others in their fields to be excellent. The two traveled to the nearby village and were dismayed to find that the obelisk was composed of poured concrete. Furthermore, the anthropologist, upon walking out behind the barn to urinate, discovered the plywood molds the farmer had used to make the obelisk, and surreptitiously took photos of them.

The professors' exposé was received, to their surprise, with derision, and our own local paper proclaimed the farmer a folk hero, running a front-page story on the man and his creation that included a large color photograph of the two. In fact, the professors' attempt to discredit the farmer only seemed to fuel his popularity. When the professors persisted in their smear campaign, a protest was staged outside their building, in which students and local residents alike demanded their dual resignation.

Mortified, the professors begged the protesters to listen to reason. They had meant no harm, they said; they only wanted to set the record straight. The farmer, after all, had lied.

The protesters, however, replied that the farmer was nice, whereas the two professors were spoilers. Upon hearing this, the professors gave up their campaign, and the protesters left them alone. Today, the farmer is a local celebrity, much loved by the residents of our county, while the professors, abhorred throughout the region, have continued their careers in much the way they had before the obelisk was discovered.

The Nuns

On a trip to the city, we took in an art exhibition that featured, among other things, a videotape of an artist painting yellow lines on the city's streets with a hand-propelled industrial line-painting machine. The lines he painted did not demarcate lanes of traffic or parking spaces; rather, they took the form of geometric designs of no apparent utility. The lines veered around stationary cars or passing pedestrians, and traced the outlines of oil stains and puddles. In an accompanying printed statement, the artist referred to the lines as "drawings." The video was filmed from a high window above the street, and the time and date flashed incessantly in the lower right-hand corner of the screen.

It happened that the artist was present at the exhibition, and he told us that not once in his years of line-painting artistry had he been caught, or even questioned, by city officials for what was clearly an act of vandalism. He said that motorists frequently asked him if they should move their cars, city workmen waved to him from trucks, and policemen appeared occasionally to direct traffic around him. His only explanation for their cooperation was the fact that he wore a hard hat and orange vest, and demarcated his "canvas" with striped sawhorses. The uniform and props carried more weight, in the onlookers' minds, than the inappropriateness of his actions.

Later that night, in a bar in Little Italy, two nuns approached carrying wicker baskets filled with dollar bills, and

153

asked us to contribute "to the St. Joseph's Orphanage." We immediately gave them two dollars apiece. As they accepted the money, the nuns said, "God bless you."

Not until the nuns had left the bar did it occur to us to question their authenticity. Once we did, however, it seemed clear that they were not nuns at all, but hoaxers dressed in rented costumes. There was a seediness about them; in fact, we seemed to recall slurred speech and bleary eyes, which suggested, in retrospect, that they were drunk. They might even have been men. This revelation ruined our evening and we left the city in a foul temper.

Days later we wondered why we had given nothing to the artist, whose performance had enlightened and amused us, while to the false nuns we had handed over four dollars. The only explanation we could come up with was that the nuns had asked for the money and the artist had not.

Short

The famous linguist came to lecture at our town's university. His speech, delivered from an illuminated lectern high on a carpeted dais, was very impressive, expanding upon some of his most profound and widely taught ideas, and many of us left the auditorium shaken to our very foundations, confident that every time we carried on a conversation we would hear as if through new ears, and understand with astonishing clarity the deep roots of our own biological, psychological, cultural and sexual realities. Every word, we were certain, would seem new.

A lucky few were invited to the cocktail party following the lecture, which was held at the monumental home of a university dean, and which the linguist was expected to attend. And in fact he did arrive, late in the evening, accompanied by his wife, a middle-aged woman of great beauty who stood almost twelve full inches above her husband. It was not that the linguist's wife was especially tall, we quickly realized, but that the linguist was unusually short.

As the evening wore on and each of us bent the linguist's learned ear, we also discovered that his voice, which had sounded imposing and clear through the auditorium's excellent sound system, was in fact small and shrill, and as the linguist accepted drink after drink from passing caterers, he began to slur his words and lapsed into Walloon, the near-extinct Belgian dialect of his childhood and occasional subject of his essays.

In the days that followed, those of us who attended the cocktail party began to see the linguist's ideas in a new light; they no longer impressed us as particularly original, and even struck some of us as obvious, the sort of ideas we ourselves might have come up with eventually if we'd just put our minds to it.

Conceptual

Our local museum, as part of its recent "Century of American Art" exhibition, commissioned a famous conceptual artist to create a large-scale work that would illustrate the state, in her opinion, of American art at century's end. The artist accepted, and began what she claimed would be a full year of research and contemplation of the work.

Meanwhile, the museum set to the tasks of choosing works from its own collection and requesting loans of seminal works from other museums around the country. A month before the exhibition was to open, the museum closed its doors entirely and renovated all its galleries. Curators prepared essays and tour booklets and hired docents to lead museumgoers through the show. Advertisements were placed which stressed the importance of the conceptual artist and her mysterious fin-de-siècle masterwork.

With a couple of weeks left before the opening of the exhibition, preparators began to hang the works in their respective galleries. The gallery devoted to the conceptual artist, however, remained empty, and she made no appearance at the museum. Curators, fearing she was ill or had (as she was known to occasionally do) suffered a nervous breakdown, left repeated messages on her answering machine. When she didn't respond, the curators visited her studio. She was never in.

One scant week before the opening, the curators received

a call from a lawyer representing the conceptual artist. He arranged a meeting with museum officials, during which he revealed that the artist would not install her great work unless a new contract was drawn up and new obligations fulfilled. These included a promise of certain foods at the opening party, a number of unusual and expensive material gifts, a poem composed in her honor to be read at an unveiling ceremony, and a substantial increase in the amount of her commission. While the museum did not wish to cave in to her demands, they nonetheless recognized the importance of her piece to their exhibition, and swallowed their pride.

On the day before the show was to open, the conceptual artist walked into the gallery reserved for her, and thumb-tacked to its far wall signed and executed copies of her original contract, her new contract, and a large color photograph of her lawyer. Then she set a metal salad bowl on the floor, filled it with twenty-dollar bills in the amount of her "raise" and burned them to ashes.

The piece drew thousands of eager museumgoers who had read about the contractual haggling and wanted to see what the fuss had been about. Reactions were strong but mixed. Some said the piece confirmed their opinion that contemporary art was an elaborate scam designed to part pretentious fools from their money. Others claimed the piece confirmed their opinion that contemporary art was once vital and incisive, but had since "sold out" to commercial interests. This latter group divided into two camps: those who believed that the new work was a perfect example of such a sellout, and those who believed that the new work was a brilliant con-demnation of those who had sold out.

At any rate, when the exhibition closed, the museum bought the controversial piece for its permanent collection, paying an undisclosed sum far above and beyond the amount originally stipulated for the work's execution.

Two Professors

I know two professors of literature who were good friends until one night, at a party, when they entered into a debate about the proper spelling of a certain word. One argued for "grey," the other for "gray." For some minutes the debate was lively and interesting. The professor who preferred "grey" believed that the word connoted a faded elegance, a kind of obsolete stateliness, which we in America commonly associate with the British; thus the British spelling, with an "e," was more appropriate. The other professor said that he could not argue with those connotations, but believed that American writers should take a stand and recontextualize the word; "gray," he insisted, was the color of the Midwestern sky, of clapboards and asphalt, and the long "a" sound in this country, less genteel and more abrasive than its British counterpart, is better expressed by the letter "a," and not the letter "e." It is worth noting that the professor who argued for "grey" was a native of the U.S., while the one who preferred "gray" had moved here from London some decades before.

As it happened, the issue was not resolved, and the debate continued for hours after everyone else had lost interest. The professors said several terrible things to one another and have not spoken in the years since the party. I have remained in contact with both, and have noticed in their correspondence that the one who previously supported "grey" has switched to "gray," and the one who liked "gray" has gone over to "grey." When I asked them about this, the first

160

explained that an extended stay in the Midwest, and exposure to its patterns of speech, convinced him of his opponent's point of view, while the second told me that his campaign to Americanize the word now seemed foolish and proud, and he was content to return to his lexicographical roots. Despite the switch, however, of which both are quite aware, the professors remain unwilling to speak to one another, though they teach in the same university department and are forced to see each other almost daily.

As for me, I now try to avoid the word entirely, and if I must describe an object in writing I tend to identify it by features other than its color.

The Hollow Door

A woman I know, a poet, moved to an apartment in a large city several years ago, in the hope that the new environment would bring a fresh perspective to her life, her enthusiasm for which had been flagging for some time. She dedicated herself to her work, and made a concerted effort, through increased correspondence, to strengthen her bonds with distant friends.

Unfortunately, things did not go her way. Her long, intimate letters went unanswered, the magazines she sent her work to never seemed to respond, and she fell into a depression. The daily mail disappointed her deeply, and often drove her to tears. She became absent-minded and failed to maintain even the simplest household responsibilities: bills went unpaid, utilities were turned off, and her refrigerator always stood empty of food.

She went on to seek solace in expensive therapy, and at long last, when her money was gone, decided to return to small town life. While preparing to move, she went to pick up the mail one day and noticed the corner of an envelope poking out of the slot. Closer examination revealed that the door was hollow, and that a letter had fallen into the open space. Extracting the letter, she discovered that the hollow extended deep into the door, and was filled with unopened mail.

In a panic, she tore the door apart with a hammer, and dozens of letters spilled onto the floor. Among them were the utility bills she never paid, generous replies to her letters, and countless responses from poetry magazines, many of them acceptances on which she had unwittingly defaulted. She spent the next day and a half on the telephone, trying to set things right with her friends and editors, and left the city not long afterward. She reports that her life is much better these days, though she still regrets not having found another way to remove the hidden mail; her landlord refused to return her security deposit (nearly eight hundred dollars) owing to the damage done to her door. She often thinks about the money and fantasizes about what she might spend it on, were it suddenly returned to her.

Impostor

A composer of film scores and musical theater found himself, despite enormous popular acclaim, smugly reviled by the critics of the day, for whose respect he nonetheless perennially longed. When he died, a biographer discovered among his papers a collection of pieces, dated in the composer's youth, that seemed to presage the difficult compositional style prevalent among other composers at the time of his death. When published, these pieces caused a great stir, as they appeared to have been dashed off and quickly abandoned for the accessible music the composer would become known and loved for.

The newly discovered music was performed to great acclaim, and, in the ensuing years, was much analyzed in academic circles, with an enthusiasm and gravity usually reserved for the greatest artists of the century. Furthermore, the more accessible works were now seen in the light of the prescient early works, and were celebrated for the very qualities that had before been the subject of such derision, since these qualities now represented a reaction against, as opposed to an ignorance of, current ideas.

For ten years the composer's reputation grew, until a critic at our local university, who had never been convinced of the authenticity of the early works, commissioned a scientific inquiry into the scores that proved they were written just before the composer died, and not in his youth, as the dates had suggested. The composer had apparently spent his declining years generating pastiches of contemporary music, then back-dated the manuscripts in order to deceive posterity.

The critic publicized his findings and wrote a revisionist biography of the composer that again reversed scholarly opinion of his work, and brought the critic his own great acclaim. It wasn't until just recently, however, that the critic's ex-lover, a former graduate student of his whom he had spurned in favor of a younger, more voluptuous and worshipful graduate student, published a paper proving that the critic's scientific inquiry was itself faked. The paper restored the composer's reputation, sullied the critic's, and propelled the ex-lover to sudden fame in academic circles. Furthermore it has resulted in the creation of an Academic Studies department at our university, dedicated to the study of study.

An investigation is apparently under way into the integrity of the ex-lover's research. The results are due to be published any day.

Mikeworld

A small South Pacific island nation of half a million, which had been colonized in the nineteenth century, suffered for many years under Spanish rule, and finally gained its independence by referendum in the late 1950s, not long ago founded its first university. Because of its size and relative poverty, the island was home to few trained academic scholars, and so when it came time for the government to select a university president, it chose a self-made intellectual and hero of the nationalist resistance effort. This man, a serious, imposing figure in his late fifties, read many hundreds of books in preparation for his job, and in addition to running the administration of the college taught a number of classes as well.

Meanwhile, the university here in our town mounted a conference on higher education in the developing world, and invited to it, among other diverse international education officials, the president of the island nation's university. He left his home with great excitement, flattered to be asked to visit a prestigious American institution, and resolved to return with new ideas for the improvement of his school.

It happens that our town is home to an interesting piece of public sculpture: a scale model of the solar system. At the city center stands a marble pedestal marked with an image of the sun that has been scaled down to the size of a basketball, and within a block are pedestals depicting Mercury,

Venus, Earth and Mars, mere specks in comparison. A few blocks away is Saturn, and several blocks more, Jupiter; the outer planets stand more than a mile from the sun.

By chance, our university's education conference coincided with an exhibition of final projects from its fine arts program, and one of these final projects, the brainchild of a goateed conceptual artist named Mike, was the construction of an additional marble pedestal. The pedestal, which the artist and his friends had installed on a patch of sidewalk somewhere between Saturn and Jupiter, documented a ringed gas giant called Mikeworld, upon which, according to an attached plaque, lived a race of sentient aliens whose enormous bodies were composed primarily of methane gas. The pedestal was identical in appearance to the ones originally commissioned by the city, and was generally thought to be very funny, except by those city officials who would eventually have to remove it.

On a break from the education conference, the university president from the island nation took to strolling about the town, and discovered, as many visitors do, the scale model of the solar system. Delighted, he resolved to walk the length of the sculpture, and inevitably he came upon the Mikeworld pedestal.

The president was not a stupid man, and his understandable initial reaction was disbelief. But because of our university's excellent reputation, and because his home island had had neither the time nor inclination to develop its own conceptual art, which he would have been hard pressed, given his cultural predisposition, to comprehend, the president decided to believe the sculpture, and returned to his country with the information that another planet existed, and it was inhabited by sentient beings.

It was not long before this information had spawned an academic mini-department of its own, and within a few years a team of astronomers on the island discovered a celestial body they thought might be Mikeworld. It was photographed and written about, and a web site devoted to it soon appeared on the Internet, where conspiracy theorists, ufologists and new age practitioners of all stripes rallied around it, and where I first encountered the blurry photographs. A hypothesis emerged about the origins of the giant gas people: they were said to be pagan gods, in retreat from the heretical techno-avarice of earth.

Eventually all this got back to Mike, the student artist, who has graduated and now works at a restaurant I visit from time to time. The pedestal has long since been removed at taxpayer expense and destroyed. When I asked him what he thinks of all the attention, he told me that he has fielded thousands of collect calls from all over the world, and though he has moved repeatedly and regularly changes his number, he is inundated daily with requests for advice, direction and money, and about once a month he receives a death threat. The hysteria surrounding Mikeworld has ruined his life, and he wishes he had never thought it up.

However, another acquaintance, an employee of the department of public works, has no sympathy for Mike, and in fact insists that the artist, having played God, has gotten exactly what was coming to him.

Meteorite

For some weeks, talk in our town focused on a meteorite that plunged to earth one morning, interrupting the prayers of the devoutly religious family into whose yard it fell. The meteorite was nearly fourteen inches in diameter, making it an unusually large specimen to have been found intact, and immediately drew the attention of our university's astronomy department. One scientist in particular, who specialized in meteors, comets and asteroids, seemed especially eager to examine the meteorite, and began negotiations with the family to acquire it for the university.

But the family was unwilling to relinquish the object, despite the small fortune the university was offering to pay for it. It seemed that they assigned to the meteorite some religious significance, and had begun to incorporate it into their devotional activities. Through it, they claimed, they were better able to speak to God.

At last the university gave up, and for days little was heard about the meteorite. But a week later, upon returning from church, the family called the police to report it missing. Within hours the meteorite was found in the scientist's lab, where he had begun to subject it to numerous tests. He was arrested, convicted and sentenced to a short prison term.

Remarkably, the scientist's defense consisted of his contention that, despite legal precedents to the contrary, the family did not own the meteorite, that in fact it was in the public domain and had been stolen from the town by the family.

Furthermore, he argued, the meteorite was being unfairly subjected to religious beliefs it did not itself hold; it was inherently an object of scientific inquiry, and its belief system was that of science alone. This defense was presented without the assistance of a lawyer.

The university, appalled by the scientist's actions and his assignation of a belief system to a meteorite, did not renew his contract for the following academic year. The family, on the other hand, has abandoned their faith and begun a new religion based on the meteorite's status as a religious artifact given to them by God. They have moved out to the country and are said to have attracted several hundred worshipers to their compound.

Lefties

A local professor was honored, and a national newspaper ran a photograph of him writing on a chalkboard before a classroom full of students. Not long afterward, the professor was asked to speak at the annual meeting of a club for left-handed persons. In his letter, the club's president explained that he had seen the photo and noticed the professor's left-handedness; he believed the professor was a credit to "lefties" and would make an inspiring and enlightening guest. Included with the letter was a booklet listing the accomplishments of left-handed people, photocopied articles asserting the creative and intellectual superiority of lefties, and a catalog of whimsical products for the left-handed, including special coffee mugs, pens, and eating utensils with pro–left-hand messages printed on them.

The professor agreed to speak to the club, and was given a large honorarium, free transportation, and a lavish hotel suite complete with mini-gym and sauna. When at last he stood before the assembled lefties, he thanked them for their invitation, then proceeded to berate them for their smugness and stupidity. He pointed out that he was, in fact, right-handed, and only appeared left-handed in the photo because the newspaper had reversed the negative; if they had looked a little more closely, he said, they would have noticed that the writing on the chalkboard was backward. He told them that they should honor others for their achievements and not their genetic circumstances, and then, only minutes into his speech, stepped down from the dais and caught a cab to the airport.

When years later the professor lost his right arm in a highway crash, he was unsurprised to receive a flood of congratulatory letters, and the first in an endless stream of free "lefty" gift items that have appeared almost daily on his doorstep ever since. Far from being angry, he views this unfortunate turn of events as a kind of poetic justice, and even tried to apologize to the lefties' club in a kind letter to its president. However, his speech had cut too deeply, and the lefties continue to bombard him with junk.

Meanwhile, the professor has learned to play a variety of left-hand pieces on the piano, and is said to be as dexterous with his left hand alone as he once was with both. He has also joined a national organization of people who have lost the use of one or more limbs, and is scheduled to speak at its next annual meeting.

7. Doom and Madness

When a local apartment fire claimed the lives of thirty-seven people, I was shocked and appalled. Later, when several residents were discovered to have been out of town, and the number of dead was revised to twenty-nine, I was somewhat relieved. At the same time, I felt faintly betrayed and disappointed, and wished that my grief and sympathy for the eight additional victims and their families had not gone to waste.

Scene

At a party we encountered a local movie critic, whose amusing and insightful column had long been the most noteworthy feature of our otherwise unremarkable daily newspaper. Late into the night, after we had all had several drinks, the critic recalled with stunning clarity a breakup scene between a man and woman which, in the film in question, had resulted in the dissolution of their family and years of financial and emotional strain for all involved. As described, the scene was characterized by high drama and superb acting, and the guests who had listened to the description all wanted to know the name of the movie. But the critic, addled either by drink or by an overabundance of film memories, was unable to remember.

Not long afterward, the critic's column was discontinued, and he began to review local restaurants instead. But his new column seemed uninspired, the prose flat, the insights into local culture and cuisine shallow and unenlightening.

It was nearly a year before I saw the critic again. He appeared tired and sick, his clothes unwashed, his skin blotchy with age. I greeted him but he did not remember me, nor did he recall the party we both attended.

A mutual acquaintance, however, passed on a rumor that the critic had begun to lose his mind. Evidently he was telling people that he had experienced all manner of implausible adventures or had known and advised certain historical figures, many of them long dead. It appeared that the critic

175

had begun to mistake events from the many films he had seen and reviewed for his own life experiences. When I related our encounter at the party, the acquaintance reported that the dramatic scene the critic described bore a strong resemblance to the man's breakup with his first wife, and the consequent domestic chaos. It appeared, then, that his madness cut both ways.

It was not long before the restaurant column was canceled as well, and replaced by a syndicated column about home decorating.

Monkeys

Strange dreams recently visited a friend, whose family- and work-related stress had long ago consigned him to regular sessions with a psychologist, which sessions, despite their short-term efficacy, seemed to have done our friend very little lasting good. In his dreams, the friend was hard at work in a familiar setting, such as his office or his home, or conducting business over the phone or via computer in a public place, like an airport or train station. For a while our friend would do this work, with little evidence to suggest the experience was a dream, until he would be startled by a volley of high-pitched cries, and look up to find that he was under attack by monkeys. The monkeys would tear at his clothes and face, inflicting terrible pain, and just as he was about to perish, he would wake from the dream, screaming at the dream-monkeys and frightening his peacefully sleeping wife. From his description the monkeys seemed to be rhesus, or some other small variety.

When our friend related these dreams to his psychologist, the psychologist asked if he had any siblings. In fact, he had: he'd been born into a large family. Were his parents divorced? Sadly, they were. The psychologist nodded. Were you ever, he asked, sexually molested as a child? Our friend replied that of course he hadn't been, that was a ridiculous suggestion. But the psychologist persisted. He believed that the monkeys represented sexual aggression; they tore at his clothes as might a rapist, and their small size made them resemble sperm. Our friend's recent anxiety, the psychologist said, had uncovered repressed memories of sexual abuse, which his tender mind had tried to disguise as monkey attacks.

Our friend gave this analysis some thought: weeks of thought, in fact, during which he became nearly incapacitated with sadness and was forced to take extended sick leave from work. What finally broke this depression was a conversation he had one night with his mother. In utter despair at what he should do with his psychologist's hypothesis, he told his mother about the dreams and asked her if she knew where they might have come from.

To his astonishment, she offered the information that, at a city zoo on his third birthday, he had in fact been attacked by monkeys. An inexperienced zoo worker had left a monkey house access door unlatched, and a pack of tiny monkeys had made a mad dash into our friend's path, causing him some minor injuries in the process. At first our friend didn't believe her, so absurd was the story, but she quickly faxed him a newspaper article on the incident, and told him that she and his father never mentioned it because it had been so upsetting for him at the time, and they didn't want to burden him further. Besides, they had had lots of children, and could spare little emotional energy on a such a (relatively) harmless occurrence, which at any rate had only affected one child among many.

Last we heard, our friend had withdrawn from his therapy and was doing somewhat, if not markedly, better in his personal and professional life. The monkey dreams have not continued.

The Names

There were six students in our school play: Jason, Heather, David, Carol, Matt and me. But in the script, which our teachers had obtained from a catalog, our characters were given other names: Scott, Jenny, Robert, Melissa, Bill and Larry. Since the oldest of us was seven, we had never before been in a play, and the difficulty of memorizing our lines was compounded by the necessity of learning new names for both ourselves and the others. For weeks we struggled through rehearsals, slowly gaining ground. Then, at the last minute, our teachers, fearing a debacle, told us to forget the stage names and simply use our own.

But our teachers had acted at the very height of our put-upon duality, and their command effected a desperate confusion, which manifested itself onstage that night as complete theatrical anarchy. We addressed one another by whatever names happened to pop into our heads, and forgot almost every scripted line, leaving our audience with only the vaguest notion of the drama's direction. The performance ended in chaos and tears, with our baffled parents applauding politely and our teachers holding their shocked faces in their hands.

Sadly, the confusion didn't end there. For weeks, we were distracted during classes, failing to respond to our teachers' direct inquiries, and were moody and unresponsive at home. When we met in the halls or on the playground, we greeted each other with incorrect names or none at all.

Most of us recovered, but Jason has married seven times, and Heather, from whom no one has heard in twenty years, is rumored to have gone mad. One lonely fall afternoon I called our local mental hospital in search of her, but was told that no patient by that name was in residence.

Crackpots

A local man, lonely and depressed due to his shyness and fear of humiliation, at long last gathered the courage to seek the advice of a psychologist, who, after listening carefully to the man's complaint, made a drastic suggestion: that the man visit a succession of public places dressed in an outlandish manner, and thus conquer his fear by immersion, much the way an infusion of a virus can inoculate a patient against disease.

The shy man was resistant at first, but in time decided that, since nothing else had worked, he would give this plan a try. First he visited the post office as Napoleon, and then the grocery store as George Washington; he attended a play as a mime, reacting to it with the appropriate exaggerated motions and facial expressions, and boarded a transatlantic airline flight dressed like a circus clown, with a multicolored wig, red nose, painted smile and giant shoes.

Soon these outings became commonplace, and the shy man was no longer afraid of them. But his day-to-day encounters with others remained strained, until he made a startling discovery: when he dressed like his psychologist— that is, in tweed jacket, round eyeglasses, brown slacks and loose necktie—he could interact freely with others. When, in addition, he grew a beard like his psychologist's, he discovered himself possessed of a deep empathy, and quickly became known to his co-workers and neighbors as a person who would listen to their problems and give clearheaded advice and sympathy. It wasn't long before he began to informally offer his services as a counselor, and soon his name and reputation had spread via word of mouth, bringing him countless clients and admirers, and a not inconsiderable amount of money. He quit his job and took on counseling full time.

Eventually the man's psychologist got wind of his patient's charade, and visited his home to confront him. Neighbors recall hearing a heated argument erupt in the hallway, and its muffled continuation behind a closed door. Hours later, a passerby reports, a man fitting the psychologist's description left the building. This man looked haggard, his hair snarled and his face bloodied, and he walked with a pronounced limp.

As it happens, the former shy man claims that it was he who was seen leaving the building, not the psychologist; he had been viciously beaten by the jealous psychologist, he says, and went out to buy first aid supplies. At that time, the former shy man maintains, the psychologist had already been gone for more than an hour. However, the psychologist has not been seen since, and foul play is suspected. Some of us believe the former shy man's story and think that the psychologist, ashamed of his behavior, did himself in; others believe that the former shy man murdered the psychologist and disposed of the body in some clever way.

There is a third group, who believe that the psychologist killed the former shy man and took his place, and in fact is now posing as the former shy man, which, given their physical similarities, is not entirely out of the question. But there is still the matter of the missing body, not to mention the implausibility of any murderer's remaining so close to the scene of the crime. This third group are thought by most of us to be crackpots, and their theory is given little credence by the newspapers or police.

New Dead

One of the odd selling points of our property here on the outskirts of town was a small graveyard, long inactive, that stood bordered by a crumbling stone wall at the top of our little hill. It belonged to the county but was surrounded by our land, and could be accessed only by a narrow dirt track, also the county's, that snaked through our land from the main road. This track was almost completely overgrown, and the cemetery itself was choked with weeds, which we tended to cut once or twice a year, out of respect for the dead, and for our own satisfaction, as we enjoyed sitting in the cemetery from time to time, contemplating the nature of life and death and listening to the sounds of the countryside.

The oldest gravestone was from 1840, and we often wondered about the dozen or so people buried there. Most had the same last name; some were children. We surmised that the dead were a family of farmers who had bravely tried, and failed, to make our rocky land yield food.

One morning the sound of a weedwhacker reached our house, and then the rumble and clank of a backhoe. Alarmed, we walked out into the woods, following the noise. It had come from the graveyard, where workmen were digging a gaping hole in the hallowed ground.

We stopped them and demanded to know what was going on. They told us that somebody new was going to be buried there. Indeed, the weeds had been cut and the road cleared, as if in preparation for a funeral.

A few days later we heard mourners walking in from the main road, and the sounds of sermonizing and grief. Not long after this, we read the dead man's obituary in the paper. As it happened, he was a member of the long-dead farm family we had imagined. However, the family weren't farmers: they were actually insane homesteaders who had killed their own children. The dead man, a descendant of a cousin of the murdered children, had for some reason requested burial there, and the county had obliged.

We walked out to the graveyard once more, to see his stone. It stood straight, gleaming and new, its engraving clear, in contrast to the crooked and worn stones of his ancestors. After that, we no longer went to the graveyard. Sometimes we heard a pickup truck rattling down the country road and leaving a few minutes later, as if someone were visiting the fresh grave. But after a while, even those visits stopped.

We no longer miss our trips to the graveyard, but all too often wonder where on our land the children were killed.

Koan

An old friend disappeared for more than ten years, then resurfaced, thinner and quieter and utterly sapped of her former vitality. She winces when spoken to and wears foam earplugs on the street. I asked her where she had been.

She told me that she had lost her mind, as a result of her graduate studies in literature, which she has permanently abandoned. Her doctoral dissertation was to have been on the "saturation hypothesis," a theory of her own devising which held that every word in a work of literature, far from having one or two most likely meanings, meant everything that any reader could make of it, and that each supposed meaning was of equal value to all others. This theory, she said, dovetailed with other current literary theories that gave more power to critics and less to writers, who tended to write with finite intentions.

However, the intensity of her study had caused her, unconsciously, to apply her theory to all words, even (and perhaps especially) those she encountered outside the realm of literature: indeed, road signs, personal conversations, song lyrics and even her own thoughts were fair game. The world swelled with meaning, and the more meaning she identified, the more she became convinced existed outside her immediate perception. Soon she had come to believe in plots against her and the presence of otherworldly interlopers in her life, and she checked in to a mental hospital for treatment. After six months, armed with a sack full of pharmaceuticals, she moved in with her sister on a farm outside our town, where she remained for nine years. Only recently has she felt confident enough to take a job downtown, and to re-enter the bustling society she is naturally drawn to.

She lives in a halfway house and relies on government subsidies to fill her prescriptions. She has given up books, music and television and taken up gourmet cooking. The world, she tells me, her eyes filled with the crazed conviction of the recently converted, is meaningless.

I see her often now, though I am neither surprised nor offended on those occasions when, unable or unwilling to admit my existence, she passes me by without saying hello.

Shelter

Our friend, the former historian, brings us this story, from the eastern European nation-state that was his area of expertise. A small city there, he tells us, was terribly besieged in the last war, and when the war was over a young man began to build a bomb shelter beneath what was left of his home. When, years later, the rest of the city was enjoying a renaissance, with great gains in public health, commerce and the arts, the man expanded and strengthened his shelter, and stocked it with all manner of food, weapons and books. Our friend met the man at this time, and asked why he looked inward when everyone else was expanding the horizons of their lives. The young man replied that he believed the current peace was unstable, and that civil unrest would soon visit their small nation.

Gradually the young man withdrew from society, and grew old. His neighbors came to regard him as mad, and as those who knew him died and new people moved to the city, his isolation became total. He was rarely seen, and when he was, adults tended to whisper to one another and children to run in fear.

But it happened that the man was right. Civil conflict did break out, and the city was mercilessly bombed for more than two months. When an uneasy peace was finally achieved, survivors visited the old man's home to request his assistance in the reconstruction effort. His house had been destroyed, but the heavy door of the shelter still stood, and they knocked loudly on it and called the man's name. The old man made no reply.

Our friend's contacts in the region described to him what happened next. The survivors, believing that the old man was ill, or perhaps that he was greedily hoarding his much-needed provisions, dug away the earth around the door, until at last they were able to pull the doorframe from the foundation. They were surprised to find that the old man was dead. He had shot himself. The shelter, on the other hand, was much as many had imagined. It was set up as a comfortable study. The walls were lined with books, and a huge store of canned food had been stockpiled beside a makeshift kitchen. The dead man sat in an upholstered armchair, a book by Tolstoy open on his lap, and the rotted remains of what must once have been a delicious meal arranged on a small table by his right elbow. A revolver lay on the floor at his feet.

There was some discussion of why the old man would have killed himself, having been so well prepared for a tragedy that had taken most citizens by surprise, but such talk quickly gave way to the work of raiding his pantry. Almost as an afterthought, the townspeople also took some of the densest-looking books, for it was spring and the branches of trees were too green and supple to be used as kindling.

Big Idea

Whether due to some degree of personal recklessness or simply to the vagaries of fortune, our friend frequently found himself in situations that brought financial ruin, emotional distress and physical injury. For some years these recurrent problems prevented him from achieving his life's goals; indeed, they left him unsure even of what those goals might be. Then, fed up at last, he returned to college to study an obscure and byzantine science he had picked almost at random, immersing himself completely in his research and quickly establishing himself among his advisors as a formidable and unusual intellect. He co-authored several influential papers with his teachers, won many honors, and was fully expected to emerge from school at the very top of his field.

For some years, however, our friend struggled to complete his doctoral dissertation. His achievements were more than sufficient to serve as the basis for an excellent paper, but he wanted to crack a particularly knotty problem that had so far eluded his superiors, and thus make the dissertation worthy not only of his degree, but perhaps even of commercial publication and international recognition.

Then, one night, in a burst of inspiration, our friend solved the crucial problem. He jotted the solution down on a few scraps of paper, worked it out in detail on his laptop computer, then left his apartment at a dead sprint to wake his colleagues at the lab.

At this moment, however, his bad luck returned, and he

was assaulted by armed thugs, who stole his computer and wallet and beat him unconscious. When he recovered from his injuries, he discovered that the weeks leading up to his inspiration had been erased from his memory by the trauma, never to be restored. Worse yet, his computer was never found, and the notes he had taken in the middle of the night made no sense to him whatsoever.

When he was released from the hospital, he returned to work, assuming that if he continued his research in the same vein that he remembered conducting it, he would again hit upon the big idea. But two years later, the solution still had not come to him. It seemed that it was not in the nature of epiphanies to be repeated. This realization so discouraged our friend that he gave up on his field entirely. Today he drives a taxi in a large Midwestern city, and keeps the cryptic notes taped to his dashboard, in the hope that their meaning will become clear again.

He is occasionally asked by his passengers about the notes. Upon hearing his story, most tell him that he shouldn't have gone out alone after dark. Our friend takes a perverse pleasure, he tells us, in dropping these people off at an inconvenient place, such as over a steaming subway grate or directly in front of a street vendor.

Live Rock Nightly

Tired by a long country drive, we stopped at a roadside tavern for a drink and something to eat. The tavern filled the first floor of a two-story brick building, and in the parking lot stood an illuminated board which read APARTMENT AVAILABLE LIVE ROCK NIGHTLY.

While eating we engaged the bartender in conversation, and discovered that he was the owner of the establishment. Emboldened by the food and drink, we brought up the reader board, suggesting that he might rent his apartment more quickly were he to remove the reference to live rock music.

The owner nodded sadly, and confessed to us that his teenage daughter had lived in the apartment once, but some years ago had died in a drunk driving accident, the result of an evening spent in another bar a few miles down the road. The owner, his eyes brimming with tears, said that he blamed himself for the accident, as he had refused to serve his daughter in his own bar, where she had been employed illegally as a cocktail waitress. With her gone, he had had to hire a legitimate waitress, and as a result the tavern was no longer profitable and had begun to lose money. Renting the apartment would make his business solvent, but he still hadn't gotten around to cleaning it out, and in fact did not want to face the task. At the same time, actively not renting the apartment was financially unjustifiable. The sign, he explained, was a compromise between his business and emotional needs. It had stood unchanged for two years,

192

even though the band had broken up and live music was no longer played here. The owner admitted that the place was about to go up for sale.

Of course we were sorry to have asked. We left the owner a large tip, though once we were out on the road, driving with extreme care, the tip struck us as a tacky, even insulting, gesture, and made us feel even worse about our rude question.

Intact

Our elderly aunt, long ago widowed, has spent the past ten years touring the world as part of an old ladies' travel club, despite a chronic social paralysis that prevents her from so much as taking the bus to the grocery store without a companion. When she returns from these distant places—which have included Thailand, Egypt, China and Brazil—and we ask her to describe her experiences, she always tells us, after some consideration, that she had a wonderful time and enjoyed the other ladies' company. She offers no other details.

At a recent family gathering, conversation lingered on a grisly subject: the crash of a commercial airliner over the Atlantic Ocean, which resulted in complete destruction of the plane and the death of all its passengers. One of us commented that such a crash constitutes a double tragedy, as the passengers lose not only their lives but their identity, because they are blown to bits and scattered in the deep ocean.

All of us were surprised when our aunt spoke up. She said that this would never happen to her. Whenever she flies, she told us, she paints her fingernails and toenails the same unusual shade of purple, to aid salvage workers in the identification of her remains. In addition, she ties a length of heavy twine to one of her toes, then runs the other end up through her slacks and blouse to her hand, where she ties it to one of her fingers. This way, if she is blown apart, the top half of her body will be tethered to the lower half, and she can enjoy a decent Christian burial more or less intact.

The silence following this revelation went on for some seconds, as we all imagined the sight of our elderly aunt's shattered corpse, held together with twine. This silence deepened when it occurred to us that she had herself imagined this very image, perhaps many times. Since then we have reinterpreted her reticence not as a symptom of some pitiable neurosis but as bold composure in the face of a morbid imagination.

Spell

A woman with whom I once worked raised two small children, whose curiosity and perceptiveness made private conversation in their presence difficult, if not impossible. Since she was rarely apart from them, she developed the habit of spelling out certain words, such as D-O-C-T-O-R or C-A-N-D-Y, to prevent them from becoming anxious or excited at inconvenient times. Eventually the children grew older and learned to spell, but my colleague continued her spelling habit, now employing it as an educational tool. She subjected the children to impromptu quizzes, asking them to point to the H-O-U-S-E or the S-T-O-P-S-I-G-N, and soon much of her speech around the children consisted of spelling.

Unfortunately, this habit spread to her speech at the office as well, and persisted long after her children had grown up and moved away. For some years she avoided any speech at all during the workday, or spoke slowly and carefully to prevent lapses. But the habit proved too strong for her, and today she spells with great frequency, presenting a new P-R-O-P-O-S-A-L or buying lunch for a C-L-I-E-N-T. The habit intensifies when she is under stress, and at these times she will occasionally grab a pen and paper and write out what she wishes to say. This compromise does seem to satisfy her urge to spell, and is easier for the listener to comprehend.

It is not unusual for her business associates to spell back at her, or even, after a long workday, to spell a word or two at home to their spouses, regardless of whether or not they have, or have ever had, children of their own.

The Mad Folder

I used to live in a large apartment building, where I had many friends, all of whom lived on the same floor as I did, and whom I'd met coming out of the elevator.

The building had twenty-two floors, but only eleven laundry rooms. This meant that those on an even floor, like me, had to share their laundry room with the people below them. But there were ample machines for everyone, and this posed no problem.

One night a neighbor of mine stopped me in the hall to tell me something. He said that about an hour before, he had moved his wet laundry to a dryer, then went out to get a bite to eat. When he came back, his dry laundry had been neatly folded and placed in his laundry basket. He was holding the basket when he told me this, and it was filled with the clean, folded laundry.

After this, many of us had a similar experience. A launderer would leave the building, or simply return to her room to watch TV, or, in one case, just pop next door to the video game room, and return to find her laundry carefully folded and stacked. This experience became a kind of joke around the floor, and we began to speak of a "mad folder." A few of the more listless among us would actually leave their laundry in the dryers on purpose, in the hope that the Mad Folder would get to it some time soon. But the Folder was unpredictable, and as often as not this labor-saving strategy was a failure. Our feeling was that the Mad Folder was a kind of random benevolence, and it was wrong to try to lure the Folder with neglected laundry. We began to think of the Folder as belonging to us, like a kind of patron saint, and we would do silly things like offer toasts or say prayers at our many cocktail parties.

One night I went into the laundry room with some dirty clothes and fell into a conversation with a woman from the floor below. While we talked, she removed some clothes from a washer and put them into a dryer. We continued talking, and at some point a distant dryer finished its cycle, and without missing a word of our discussion she crossed the room, removed the laundry and began to fold it.

I asked her if that was more of her own laundry she was folding, and she said that it wasn't. She told me that she liked folding laundry, it calmed her and she enjoyed imagining strangers discovering their folded clothes. She said she did it all the time.

I invited her back to my apartment and one thing led to another. For several days we carried on, calling in sick to work and making love at all hours. Lying by my side in my bed one night, the Mad Folder told me that she was glad to have met me when she did, because she was not getting on so well with her roommate and in fact was planning on moving out of the building. Did I mind if she stayed with me for a few days? Since our affair had been nearly unceasing and was conducted exclusively at my place anyway, I agreed to her plan.

That was a mistake. I came back from work the next day to find all my clothes washed and folded and put away in my drawers. Furthermore, the bed was neatly made and my closet rearranged and organized. My books had been alpha-betized and kitchen implements sorted and secreted in the cabinets; and the refrigerator, purged of its rotting food and scoured clean, looked almost completely empty.

I told the Mad Folder that it wasn't working out, and after a terrible fight—I had, after all, promised to let her stay—she stormed out, never to be seen again.

When I told my friends what had happened, they refused to believe it. Then the folding stopped. At first, our relation-ships went on as they had before my affair: in fact, our so-cializing seemed to intensify, as if in compensation for our loss. But soon the Folder's disappearance began to take its toll. In the hallway, conversations stopped abruptly when I appeared. The laundry room took on a new desolation, and people walked around in wrinkled clothes. Eventually I spied several floormates doing their laundry two floors away, in a foreign laundry room.

That ought to have been my cue to move away, but instead I haunted the laundry rooms each night for weeks, folding whatever dry laundry I found. This continued until a woman caught me folding her underwear, and I was informed that if I didn't put it down immediately, she would call the super to beat me up.

Until I left the city for good, I did my wash at laundro-mats, a different one every week.

Sickness

A friend of ours lost a small child to a terrible disease. So awful was this illness, and so prolonged the child's death, that his wife suffered a nervous breakdown and, since she and our friend had ample money for professional help, checked herself into a spa to recover. She asked our friend, however, to remain at their palatial home and eradicate all traces of the child's existence. Such was the depth of her grief. When he had completed this task he was to contact her, and she would return. We spoke to him at the time and he seemed confident that he would finish quickly.

However, the job was not as simple as he had anticipated. He had no trouble dispatching baby toys and clothes, photographs and crayon drawings. He hired a cleaning service to rid the house of the child's smell. But it quickly became evident that items less directly involved with the child nonetheless stirred up painful memories, and he had to dispose of these as well: his own clothes, upon which the child had spit up; their furniture, on which she had played and slept; the car that had ferried her to and from the hospital; the kitchen appliances, which they used to prepare her meals. It wasn't long before our friend was having the floors removed and the lawn and shrubs torn up. We saw him very infrequently during this period. Though he was compelled by what obviously had become a kind of sickness, he always looked clean and neat, doggedly on his way somewhere related, no doubt, to his mission.

Just recently we noticed that a wrecking ball was at work knocking down our friend's house, and bulldozers were chugging across the property, flattening the landscape. We have also heard from our friend's wife. She checked out of the spa within a month and in time divorced our friend, for which we can't blame her, given that she would likely have found herself on our friend's list of things to eliminate. She has remarried and is planning on starting a new family.

Our letters and phone calls to our friend are not returned. Once we baby-sat for the doomed child, in the days before she grew ill, and it seems likely that we are regarded as too closely affiliated with her memory. This suits us well, however, as it seems possible that our friend, if given the opportunity, might kill us.

Unlikely

M., once our close friend, gradually became unbearable as her life's disappointments led to bitterness, finger-pointing and crude gossip. We took our time returning her letters and phone calls, finally refusing to answer them at all, and eventually the letters and calls stopped entirely.

Then, just when we thought we would never again hear from her, she contacted us with the terrible news that she had been diagnosed with cancer, and was beginning treatment immediately. Horrified, we apologized for our past inattentiveness to her problems, promising to stay in close touch during her time of need. It seemed to us now that our complaints about her personality had been petty and perhaps even inaccurate; indeed, it was hard to remember exactly what we had found so unappealing about this friend, whose bravery in the face of death revealed her as a woman of strong, even extraordinary, character.

After a battle of several years, M. succeeded in defeating the cancer, and her doctors reported with pleased surprise that the disease was unlikely to recur. We sent her a large fruit basket in congratulation, accompanied by a letter expressing our gratitude for her years of loyal friendship.

However, our friend's restored health did little to prevent further personal and professional failures, which amassed in much the way they had before she was sick, and she again resorted to monotonous grumbling, accusation and slander. Once again she became difficult to bear, and again we cut

her off, more confident than ever in the rightness of our reaction, even going so far as to surmise that her illness may
have been the result not of random misfortune or genetic
error but of her own bad habits, such as smoking, overeating
and indolence. When recently we learned through the grape-
vine that she had suffered a relapse and was not expected to
survive, we were saddened, but remained convinced that such
a thing was unlikely to happen to us.

Smoke

A house to the west of ours cannot be seen from our windows, as it stands in a shallow depression surrounded by tall trees. But it is possible to observe, on cold mornings, the woodsmoke that rises from the house and disperses in the air. Since my study faces west, I have a good view of the neighboring property, and for years, when I found it difficult to concentrate or needed to relax, I would gaze out the frosted window at the endlessly rising and vanishing white smoke.

One winter morning some years ago, while watching the smoke rise from the trees, I noticed an abrupt change in its quality. It turned blue and then black, varying in volume from a thin plume to a heavy cloud, and back again. I studied the shifting smoke for the better part of an hour before returning to my work.

It wasn't until a week later that our neighbor was arrested for murder. She had used a shotgun to kill her abusive husband and—with the help of her two children, an ax and a saw—chopped his body into pieces, then burned the pieces in the woodstove. The bone chips that remained were dropped down the outhouse pit. To my horror, the neighbor identified the morning I had been watching as the time of her crime. She is now in prison, and her children are under the care of foster parents and several psychologists.

New owners gutted the house, which sold for next to nothing, and furnished it with a fireplace where the woodstove, removed by police as evidence, once stood. White smoke has again appeared on the horizon. Consequently, I have installed a shade on my study window, which I pull down on cold mornings to obscure the sky. Only in summer do I raise the shade completely.

Flowers

We met an acquaintance on the street looking uncharacter-istically glum. His face, usually animated and friendly, had become frozen into an attitude of misery, a condition all the more surprising because he had recently married a beautiful and intelligent woman, and had seemed deliriously happy in the immediate wake of the wedding.

Over drinks, our friend told us his tragic story. He had courted his wife with relentless abandon in the months after they met, and when it came time to ask her to marry him, he bought a gigantic bouquet, which he presented to her as he proposed. So eager was he to hear her accept his pro-posal, and so ardent was his love, that, without a moment of forethought, he promised to bring her flowers every single day they were married, should she say yes. Of course she ac-cepted, and they were wed some months later.

The first weeks of their marriage were an unadulterated joy. They honeymooned in Italy in the spring, and every morning he rose early, went out and bought a bouquet, which he gave to her while she still lay in bed. The morn-ing they left for home, he was too rushed to buy flowers, but their plane arrived in America with ample time to spare, and he bought her a rose at the airport. Upon their return to our city, he found a florist near the house they shared, and vis-ited there every morning before the two left for work.

Soon, however, his office schedule was changed. He had to report to work an hour earlier than usual, well before the florist opened, and got off at half-past five, the very moment the florist closed. To get around this problem, he sometimes visited the florist on his lunch hour or, barring that, dropped in at the market on his way home. The resulting flowers were often less than fresh, but still fulfilled his promise.

When he went away to a business conference, he arranged to have flowers delivered to his wife at home each morning, and when his wife went away to visit her sister in a faraway town, he had them delivered to her there. But he was beginning to see how complicated life could be under this system, even in the best of times, and he found himself beset by worries that he would forget, or that, for some reason, cut flowers would suddenly become unavailable in our region. Then there were some close calls: a hectic day that ended with his snipping a rose from a bush in a public park; an evening of endless business meetings after which, near midnight, he brought her a plastic flower arrangement from his secretary's desk; and a dreadful near-collapse that concluded with a fax of a drawing of a flower.

After this last, he began to tire of his promise, and brought the flowers in the most unromantic, offhand manner, plucking a few dandelions or a clump of clover from the yard on his way into the house, and once returning from the market with a sack of pastry flour and handing that to her, as a kind of awful pun. He began to hate himself for his weakness; and though his wife had many times told him that he needn't adhere to the promise, she now began to resent his disrespectful, passive-aggressive tone, and fights ensued. One night they actually began shoving one another around, and the next day his wife filed for divorce.

While the divorce was pending, our friend sent daily bouquets of absurd proportions to his wife's new apartment, accompanied by little cards printed with insults and vulgarisms, and on the day the divorce went through, he sent her one hundred black roses. The roses nearly wiped out his savings, and when he went snooping around her place that night, to see if she was having an affair, he found the hundred roses lying in the dumpster out back, along with the gigantic ornate vase they came in.

Our friend has since realized that she would have married him anyway, without the promise, a thought that pains him terribly. But, he says, he takes some small comfort in knowing that he did indeed keep his promise, and that, though deeply lonely, he is a man of unswerving dedication, which is not something most people can say about themselves these days.

Heirloom

I remember deer hunting with my father when I was a young man. He always carried the same antiquated rifle, its stock and trigger worn from use. Once he pointed out the nearly obliterated remains of a carved set of initials, and he told me the rifle had belonged to his own father, who killed himself when my father was still a boy. In fact, he said, the suicide was committed with this very rifle.

It wasn't until I was much older that I realized how horrifying this revelation was, so horrifying that I later convinced myself I had made the whole story up.

When my father shot himself, I inherited the rifle. By now I had a child of my own, but I had given up hunting in the fall. I put the rifle, along with some other possessions of my father's I couldn't bear to sell, into a self-storage warehouse outside town.

At those times when my unhappiness becomes most difficult to bear, I drive out to the warehouse and stare at the gray corrugated-steel door my father's things are stored behind. This never fails to improve my mood. I don't bring the key on these excursions, of course; I haven't seen the key in years and would be hard pressed to tell you where it is.

Brevity

A local novelist spent ten years writing a book about our region and its inhabitants which, when completed, added up to more than a thousand pages. Exhausted by her effort, she at last sent it off to a publisher, only to be told that it would have to be cut by nearly half. Though daunted by the work ahead of her, the novelist was encouraged by the publisher's interest, and spent more than a year excising material.

But by the time she reached the requested length, the novelist found it difficult to stop. In the early days of her editing, she would struggle for hours to remove words from a sentence, only to discover that its paragraph was better off without it. Soon she discovered that removing sentences from a paragraph was rarely as effective as cutting entire paragraphs, nor was selectively erasing paragraphs from a chapter as satisfying as eliminating chapters entirely. After another year, she had whittled the book down into a short story, which she sent to magazines.

Multiple rejections, however, drove her back to the chopping block, where she reduced her story to a vignette, the vignette to an anecdote, the anecdote to an aphorism, and the aphorism, at last, to this haiku:

Tiny Upstate town
Undergoes many changes
Nonetheless endures

Unfortunately, no magazine would publish the haiku. The novelist has printed it on note cards, which she can be found giving away to passersby in our town park, where she is also known sometimes to sleep, except when the police, whose thuggish tactics she so neatly parodied in her original manuscript, bring her in on charges of vagrancy. I have a copy of the haiku pinned above my desk, its note card grimy and furred along the edges from multiple profferings, and I read it frequently, sometimes with pity but always with awe.

Some of the stories in this collection originally appeared in *3rd Bed, Best American Short Stories 2005, Bookpress, CutBank, Denver Quarterly, Epoch, Fox Cry Review, Granta, Harper's Magazine, LitRag, McSweeney's, Night Rally, Santa Fe Review,* and *Southeast Review,* as well as on the radio shows *Weekend America* and *Selected Shorts.*

J. ROBERT LENNON is the author of seven novels, including *Familiar, Castle,* and *Mailman.* His stories have appeared in the *Paris Review, Granta, Harper's, Playboy,* and the *New Yorker.* He lives in Ithaca, New York, with his wife and two sons, and teaches writing at Cornell University.

The text of *Pieces for the Left Hand* is set in Adobe Garamond Pro. Book design by Rachel Holscher. Composition by BookMobile Design and Publishing Services, Minneapolis, Minnesota. Manufactured by Versa Press on acid-free paper.